M.K. GILROY

RISE
OF THE
BEAST

THE PATMOS CONSPIRACY
BOOK 1

M.K. GILROY

RISE
OF THE
BEAST

THE PATMOS CONSPIRACY
BOOK 1

SYDNEY
LANE
PRESS

Published by Sydney Lane Press, a Division of Gray Point Media LLC.
2000 Mallory Lane, Suite 130-229
Franklin, Tennessee 37067
www.sydneylanepress.com

EDITIONS
Paperback: 9780975866221
E-Book: 9780975866238

Library of Congress Control Number: 2016937545

International English Language Version

Dedicated to my lovely and loving wife, Amy

Acknowledgments

Special thanks to early manuscript reviewers who provided
invaluable feedback on bringing the beast to life!
My heartfelt thank you to Allen Deaver, Bob DeMoss,
Sid Frost, Brian Henson, Lanny Hester, Julie Jayne,
Danny McGuffey, Kim Russell, David Sams, and Jeane Wynn!

M.K. Gilroy Novels

The Kristen Conner Mystery Series
Cold As Ice
Cuts Like a Knife
Every Breath You Take
Under Pressure – Coming August 2016

The Patmos Conspiracy
The Rise of the Beast–Book 1
Voice of the Dragon – Book 2 – Coming Fall 2016
Mark of the Beast – Book 3 – to be announced
The Blood Red Horse – Book 4 – to be announced
The Final Battle – Book 5 – to be announced

Just Before Midnight: A Christmas Eve Novella

I, John, both your brother and companion in the tribulation and kingdom and patience of Jesus Christ, was on the island that is called Patmos for the word of God and for the testimony of Jesus Christ. I was in the Spirit on the Lord's Day, and I heard behind me a loud voice, as of a trumpet.

Revelation 1:9-10, NLT

Patmos is a small, lightly populated Greek island in the Aegean Sea. Christian tradition identifies it as the place where the Apostle John was banished by the Roman government, and the place where he received the Revelation of Christ. The Cave of the Apocalypse is a popular destination for Christian pilgrims.

Book 1

Rise of the Beast

Then I stood on the sand of the sea. And I saw a beast rising up out of the sea, having seven heads and ten horns, and on his horns ten crowns, and on his heads a blasphemous name.

Revelation 13:1, NLT

Prologue

From the Journal of Jonathan Alexander

Some things are true but can't be said out loud.

I learned that lesson the first time I told my dad he was a drunken bum. My dad wasn't so bad. He wasn't a mean drunk. I simply shouldn't have spoken the truth of his miserable existence when he was sober. That's when he got mean.

Western Civilization is dying. That means the death of invention, productivity, learning, beauty, and peace—at least an acceptable level of peace. Total peace is not in the best interests of progress.

The death of Western Civilization means no more rule of law. I have not always followed the law, but I respect the law.

What will the world be like when the only quarter of humanity that brings value to human existence gives way to the savages?

The direction the world is traveling must be stopped, no matter what it takes or what the cost.

See, I told you some things are true but can't be said out loud. I can see your revulsion to what I write. I can picture the uncomfortable flicker of your eyes. You want to turn away from me.

But be honest. Confess what you know to be true in your heart. Deep down, you feel a glimmer of recognition ... maybe even a twinge excitement, don't you? Somewhere beneath the veneer of political correctness and feigned compassion, you can almost feel and believe that which is authentic in my words. Can the world continue as it is and be home to a thriving civilization?

You know the answer. The world cannot continue on its present demographic course. The exponential aggregate of population growth alone is unsustainable. I feel a twinge of sadness that some must die for no other reason than the profligacy of their forebears. I feel no sadness for the necessary deaths of others. If not eradicated, the global death throes created by brutal peoples and cultures that offer nothing of beauty, will be horrific.

You are looking away. I make you uncomfortable. I don't blame you for not approving my words. You would be labeled a bigot, selfish, arrogant, barbaric, and even ignorant. All the while, barbarians create and perpetuate a world of brutality within the sphere of their ugly self-destructive existence.

I am not the only one who believes the death of the West means a plunge into unfettered barbarism for the world. Many see the same truth and know that something must be done, but shrink back from the required confrontation in thought and deed. I'm sure some believe that benevolence and education will transform cultures of misery into enlightened beacons of hope in dark lands. I don't criticize that sentiment. The world needs kindness, however naïve, misguided, and inefficacious it might be.

But those who recognize the inescapability of what is happening and yet choose to do nothing, bear guilt. They are cowards who have no taste for the necessary steps to save what is good in the world in order to give hope to the future. Their only comfort will be that their mortal existence—their only existence—will pass away before the full measure of impending calamity has materialized. But what of their children and grandchildren?

I've lived a reasonably long life. There is nothing more for me to attain. So why do I choose to undertake what is nearly impossible now? Well, someone must. The Creator God, if he exists, certainly doesn't seem interested in the world condition at the moment, nor for quite some time.

You will, of course, accuse me of insanity and evil. I say the same of you. You have fallen under the spell of the Sophists, those clever thinkers and influencers who parse minutiae while blind to seismic events and realities right before their eyes. You can no longer recognize what is good and evil. You could never understand that it is hope and truth that drives me. Am I wrong to believe that perhaps Alaric has not yet crossed the Tiber with his savages and breached the wide-open gates of Rome? Perhaps there is more time to save civilization.

With the moral dissipation of the West, that time is short.

I see your eyes. You look at me as if I am a madman. You somehow believe that everything will work out despite the present course. Do the math. Compare the existence of those having babies with those not having babies. Do you not see that the numbers of the savage and deficient are swelling to flood and subdue the lands of prosperity and progress?

You may wish to cling to your belief that no one has the right to affirm cultural superiority and judge peoples that offer nothing but pain and suffering. But who is the madman?

Who will speak the words that must be spoken? Who will perform the deeds? In the same manner as the Greek and Roman Empires of my heritage, the Western Civilization we know now has been robbed of its faith and courage. Just as the Sophists were the bedfellows of death, decay, and ruin for my forefathers in Athens, so the Sophists of today play with fanciful and irrelevant notions of progress while the world burns around them. Even now the swirling smoke from the flames blinds them and the lemmings who follow them obediently over the cliff and into the abyss of the new and final dark ages.

Western Civilization is all that has really mattered in world history. Let the sheep of academia bleat of an enlightened fragment of a parchment or a single mathematical discovery or a shard of painted ceramic or an etching on a stone from other societies. I'm happy to recognize and give credit to the achievements and wonders of other world cultures. But deep down everyone knows Western Civilization has spawned the only world history that matters for a simple reason. No other culture, no other ethos, no other philosophy has created the pathway for the poor to create a middle class and for a burgeoning middle class to become rich—and for all to live with some modicum of decency.

Think of that truth before judging me for what I am about to do. Test my words against all you know. Art, learning, and prosperity for the masses is unique to the ideals founded in Athens. Hate me if you will, but were I to shrink from the voice inside of me, you would learn soon enough there is no such thing as a noble savage.

In the past one hundred years the West's engine of upward mobility has done its work so well that even its own poor feel they are deserving of more than they are able to attain by their own sweat and guile while they already have much more than all but the wealthiest of the other world cultures, simply because of where they live and the men of courage and willfulness who built it. I want to look in their eyes and laugh when the teats of largesse and abundance dry up.

When Socrates raised the bitter cup of hemlock to his lips, the city elders of Athens watched but did not understand what was really happening. They were not witnessing the death of a wise man but of wisdom. As they killed truth, they ordained their own death.

The world is dying before our eyes and the ones who can do something to save what is decent and beautiful in humanity refuse to act. They know not that they drink deeply from Socrates cup. They dance with the devil in his many forms and forget that he will exact his due.

The world needs an intercessor, whether with God or Lucifer or the sum of man's belief in something divine.

On the Island of Patmos, the place of my father's birth, St. John the Apostle had a vision of a beast rising from the sea.

What is needed today is a beast. So I have prayed to the Creator God, whether he lives or listens or exists only as a projection of human wishing. I have told him that I will do what all others fear to do. Perhaps if he exists, he will be pleased that one man has stood up to fight. The God of the Bible did flood the Earth and drown the wicked after all. He has not always sat idly by while the world falls into ruins, though I suspect he has always lacked the power or the will to do what is necessary for his children to enjoy and master the dangerous world in which he placed them.

I will seek his favor. If he denies me his blessing, I will do what others before me have done. I will bend his will to my will.

I have not lost my courage … I have not lost my will to rule … I will rise from the sea. I will ride the blood red horse of the Apocalypse. I will be the Beast who destroys the world in order to save it.

1

Jersey City, New Jersey

BURKE HAD DONE THE ROUTINE a thousand times. Ten thousand times. Raise the gun, set the site on the center of the torso or head—the correct placement of a kill shot is always situational—and pull the trigger.

The Heckler and Koch 45 caliber handgun weighed just over two pounds. The kickback was manageable. Many inexperienced shooters opted for 40 caliber or 9mm handguns, following the logical but false assumption that a smaller load meant less recoil. Burke fought with the Desert Eagle 50 caliber in Afghanistan and Iraq—recoil was not an issue for him. Lean and muscular, highly trained and naturally skilled, the weight and kickback of the HK45 was no problem.

His target was ninety feet away. He lifted the gun, opted for a headshot, and squeezed the trigger. The roar of the discharge created no loss of aim for Burke. The barrel pulled up and left; to be expected. But with right arm ramrod straight, left arm slightly bent to provide stability for the classic two-handed shooting stance, he made the subtle adjustment of his site line, firmed his hold, pulled the trigger, and discharged nine more bullets in less than five seconds. He was confident he fired ten kill shots.

Burke flipped the switch and a chain rattled as it pulled the small target to him. There was only one hole in the head, four centimeters in diameter. All ten cartridges had zeroed in on the same spot. He shot a squirrel with a .22 at a more than a hundred-yard range when he was eight. He still had the master marksman's gift of physical calm in the midst of a violent explosion.

And he needed it now. He was nervous. If he were personally out on the front lines of a dangerous operation, he would be fine. But putting an amateur into the battlefield—and knowing this was D-Day—was grating across his nerves like nails on a chalkboard.

She was perfect for what needed to be done. But she was in over her head. She knew what she was getting into, I told her myself, he repeated in his mind for the thousandth time.

I didn't sugarcoat any of the risks. I was completely honest with her.

But he knew better. Is it honesty if the person you are speaking to cannot truly fathom the meaning of your words? Concepts like danger and risk aren't visceral when discussed in a coffee shop. You don't go up against the kind of adversary they were facing if you really knew the danger. You would have to be a fool.

What does that make me?

When fighting a monster, all of us are amateurs, all of us are in over our head, he thought.

Tall and slender, generously endowed, full lips, large hazel eyes flecked with golden amber, creamy skin, high check bones, thin aquiline nose, luxuriant honey-colored hair—a beauty queen—she was not without natural defenses ... nor weapons. Could she pull off what he tasked her to do? He would know soon enough.

Another thought gnawed at him no matter how hard he willed it to slink back into the darkness of his subconscious. He liked her. He wanted her to be okay. He wanted to know her. He somehow sensed she was his path back to decency. This was certainly no time for sentiment, but there it was, refusing to surrender to his iron will.

Maybe his feelings were simple biological reaction to her feminine allure.

You can't think like that and survive in this business, he repeated to himself. Again.

He pinned a new target to the holder, hit the switch to send the chain rattling away, popped the spent magazine from the handle of the Heckler, and jammed a fresh spring-loaded holder with ten more rounds in his German designed instrument of death.

The mathematical law of regression to the mean suggested his next ten shots would not be as accurate as his marks from the first magazine. But laws were meant to be broken. When he took a surreptitious glance behind him at the viewing window, he saw that he had attracted a small group of spectators—not what he wanted, but he might as well put on a show.

He racked the first bullet in the chamber, switched to a one-handed stance, and squeezed off ten rounds. He was certain the new target would come back with ten shots clustered in a single hole.

So why keep practicing? Why not? What else am I going to do while I wait except go crazy?

The chain clattered back with a target bearing a four-centimeter hole in the chest. He wadded it up and dumped it in the trash can. He broke the Heckler and Koch down and cleaned it carefully, pushing the bristle brush in and out of barrel. He laid the polymer frame gently in the hard shell carry case. He walked over to the corner of shooters alley, picked up the broom, and swept the spent shell casings into a dustbin. He exited the two doors leading to the lobby, took off the Howard Leight earmuff set, and nodded quickly at a few gawkers. He kept his eye contact to a split second, announcing he wasn't in the mood to socialize.

"Nice shooting," the kid working behind the ammunition counter remarked.

Burke just nodded, running a hand through dark hair, cut short, the first hints of white on his temple.

"We finally got the Federal Hydra Shok back in stock, if you need any ammo," the kid continued, trying to engage. "It's about impossible to get lately, but I've got a case stashed in the back."

Burke turned back and said, "I'll take six boxes," peeling three 100 dollar bills from his gold money clip with the 7th Ranger Regiment insignia onlay—a rare souvenir of his past life. Would he ever use the over-the-counter bullets? Only at a range. In real life, his ammo was custom made.

"Were you Army?" the kid asked. "Where'd you learn to shoot like that?"

Questions were why it was better to not draw attention.

"My dad was a marksman and taught me," Burke lied.

He quickly exited the storefront, put the gear in the trunk of his rented Chevy Malibu, and pushed the button to start the car.

I did tell her the truth of what she as getting into. So why do I feel so empty?

2

Northern Yemen

NICKY WANTED TO VOMIT AT what he witnessed. The only redeeming quality of the executions was watching the American put up a hellacious fight. Nicky had to hand it to the man. He did not die quietly.

The young Saudi prince was a whole different matter. He was surprisingly pliant. Stoic? At peace? In shock? He accepted the blade with nothing but a blank, expressionless, stare, with only a single flare of his smoldering onyx eyes as the executioner touched the scimitar to his neck to mark where he would sever the man's head with a savage stroke of power and grace.

The Saudi was the son of a powerful Wahhabi sheikh. He was the model for the "new Arab man." Intelligent, savvy, urbane, but ever faithful to Allah. Even after earning degrees from the Sorbonne University in Paris and Heidelberg University in Germany, he was still a true believer; maybe more of a believer after experiencing firsthand the empty decadence of the West. Nicky knew that the sheikh's son had despoiled more than a few virgins in his student days, but he had eschewed the drug and party scene that seemed requisite on the resume of a wealthy heir to an oil fortune.

The prince's father, Sheikh Sulaymon, was not a billionaire, but close enough. His fury and vengeance would be colossal when he discovered that his eldest son, his beloved son, his anointed son, had been slaughtered by a toothless, barbaric, drug-addled, two-bit rival.

The American was far from stoic. He was obviously not anticipating immediate entrance into paradise with a bevy of eager virgins awaiting him.

He was strong, a demon with his hands, and he fought frantically and loudly to keep them free. He administered at least two broken wrists, one oozing, dripping eye socket, and a crushed larynx to the men who ultimately overpowered him. He bellowed and roared in the night as testimony to the survival instinct.

But unlike scripted scenes in action movies, there is no choreography in a real life fight that presents one combatant at a time to be dispatched by spins, jumps, kicks, and fists, administered in artistic arcs and jabs. A fight is messy business. Put enough bodies, enough weight, enough flesh, enough fists and boots on one man and he will buckle and fall.

Even on the ground, his hands bound, his muscles spent and trembling like gelatin, the American mustered enough energy for one last head snap to break Sheikh Malmak's nose.

There's a reason you have bodyguards and other underlings taste your food for poison and fight your battles, Nicky thought. But out of pride the sheikh insisted on looking into the eyes of the American to let him know he was defeated.

The broken nose was no real matter in the long run. The Sheikh was a hideously ugly old bird, with a missing ear, a mouth full of qat-stained rotten, broken teeth, and a misshapen mole the size of a euro coin that sprouted a menagerie of black and bristly white hairs. A half-smashed nose wouldn't be the reason he didn't make the cover of GQ. Not even the Yemen edition.

Malmak's name meant *highness*. The sheikh was pleased when the Saudi minister of religious affairs made it illegal for parents to name a baby boy Malmak anymore, a prohibition that migrated to Yemen.

He was pleased because he believed that when history recounted his exploits, his name, Malmak, would be less diluted by smaller men. Nicky got all that through his translator who might or might not be reliable.

Malmak. Highness. A great name, but the bearer was not destined for the history books. Pride precedes the fall, Nicky mused.

Don't fall in the same trap. A mad sheikh in pain might be enough to get you killed before you get out of this cesspool. Uncle told me to delegate more. Beginning tomorrow, if there is a tomorrow for me, I will listen.

The American was spent. His legs and hands and waist were bound to a chair with duct tape. He got one last bite to the shoulder of the soldier circling him with the dull metal adhesive. Blood dripped from his mouth. Was it a chunk of meat from Azam, the guard he bit, or his own blood?

The video camera was on a tripod ten feet in front of him. The executioner was ready. In one single blow, the Saudi's head had separated from his neck, fallen with a thud to the ground, and then rolled on the dusty, rocky ground, spewing a jet of blood. That took real strength—and a sharp blade that the executioner tended to with a gentleness that belied its ceremonial purpose in Malmak's tribe.

The American would not be given a clean death. Because of the broken nose the sheikh had ordered the obese mute to use his dullest blade on the American. This was going to take time; it would be gory. Nicky knew better than to turn his head or avert his eyes. He had orchestrated the executions and now his job was to be strong, to watch every hack of nothing more than a dull, rusty machete, as it went through veins, muscles, arteries, tendon, and bone.

The American lifted his head, spat blood, and cursed the sheikh. Nicky almost laughed.

What a fighter.

The dull gray blade slashed sideways, but not with the force and length of stroke that killed the handsome young Arabian prince. Nicky felt blood splatter on his face, as the metal dug into the neck about a fourth of the way through. Not deep enough to decapitate or kill the man.

The American glared, snarled, and bellowed but no clear words emerged, no more profanity and curses filled the air.

He would fight to the end. Nicky would like to have known him. If he had, he would have found another patsy to play the role of a treacherous American operative in this bloody charade.

A second slash of the blade landed with a little more authority but the American somehow ducked into it and lost an inch of scalp and flesh on the top of his head for his efforts. The moon and firelight showed an eerie, gleaming white patch of skull. The man's mouth was wide open in pain and rage, but it was a silent scream.

Nicky nearly gagged from the assaultive stench as the man voided his bowels and bladder.

What was his name? I should remember. He deserves that much.

So much blood. The American couldn't last much longer. Just don't look away. Show no weakness. Nicky could feel the testosterone surging through the campsite. A laugh to his left. An excited shriek to his right. A chorus of undulating voices from all sides.

Don't turn from the main show. Eyes straight ahead. Don't flinch. Watch. Smile. Maybe let out a yell. Be one with them. And perhaps you will live another day.

The third stroke broke through the vertebrae deep enough that it stuck tight in a chunk of cartridge. The executioner, sweat roiling between the swells of his saggy chest and down his enormous belly, had to give several violent tugs to free the blade. Nicky had seen lots of blood—had caused lots of blood—but his stomach gave a violent wrench at the sight of the strands of bright red meat, appearing freakishly like the frayed end of a rope, spilling from the top and bottom of the gash. The ground around the American was now pooled in blood. His body continued to twitch and jerk—his brain might already be dead but his electrical impulses were still looking for a fight. Any physical movement was nothing but unspent energy racing through nerve patterns.

The American fought a heck of a fight. His head still clung to his body on the fourth stroke, maybe by nothing more than skin. What a way to die. It was contagious in this part of the world. But dead was dead. Was the prince any better off for a clean death? What was a minute or two of less suffering he experienced than the American? Both would still be dead forever.

Nicky was in the process of delivering more than twenty-five million US dollars in weaponry to this obscure tribe in northern Yemen, not far from the border of Saudi Arabia. As the handoff approached, he had used an unwitting conspirator in his Middle East network to plant the story of a rival tribe—the Wahhabi tribe controlled by the prince's father, Sulaymon—coordinated by the American CIA of course, which planned to steal the weapons from Malmak.

The American wasn't CIA—at least not to Nicky's knowledge—but he was big, athletic, and just happened to be negotiating a deal with the Wahhabi tribe to bring a stable electrical grid to the Hadhramaut Valley, a project the handsome Saudi prince had been working on since his return from the West. The output of his father's oil wells was more than sufficient to improve the lot of the region the tribe inhabited.

With the way the man fought, Nicky mused, maybe the American was CIA. Nonetheless, he and the prince's protestations of innocence fell on deaf ears. The two men had simply been in the wrong place at the wrong time when Malmak's men kidnapped them. Nicky felt a little bad for his part in their brutal ending, but he knew it was for a greater good. His uncle would be pleased.

That was the beauty of the plan. Arm men with long-standing grievances and up-to-date bad intentions, then spread rumors that their historical enemies have even more nefarious plans to inflict on them, and your work was mostly done for you. Passionate flames of emotion that turned intentions into actions quickly raced out of control and the next thing you knew you were watching an elegant Wahhabi prince's head bounce and roll. Once the first shot was fired— or the first head rolled—a response would always follow. In the case of the prince's father, it would be a much greater response that would echo throughout the region, turning tribe against tribe.

With what we just gave Malmak, I give him a month rather than a week to survive the storm coming his way. The fool thinks he can win. Keep encouraging that thought. The only reason he will live out the year is that Sulaymon will keep him alive to torture him.

The Americans were weak at the moment and might not acknowledge the death of one of their citizens. But whether or not they had boots on the ground, they and their allies were enmeshed in the region and would be involved in the ensuing battles one way or another. Particularly if the battles spread to the territories of their allies who helped keep their energy costs inexpensive.

Malmak was foolish to think his ragtag, near destitute little tribe could wreak the damage he thought they could, no matter how many weapons Nicky supplied to them. But with Malmak's righteous passion and enormous ego, Nicky was certain the bloodshed that would follow would be a good return on investment.

This moment, this incident was a carefully scripted scenario to measure impact. He wondered if it was even necessary.

The ISIS campaign in Syria and Iraq was not completely organic, but even with very little outside nudging, its exponential growth was nothing short of amazing. What Nicky was accomplishing—and he was not sure how much credit he could take—was significant, his uncle told him. Nothing pleased Nicky more than his uncle's approval.

It was time for the killing to spread south and east on the Arabian Peninsula, to Saudi Arabia, Yemen, and on into the Emirates. Work was already underway to turn brother against brother in Egypt. Fighting in Syria had taken on a life of its own and was already spreading to Iraq,

Turkey, and Lebanon. Russian arrogance—*they forget their wasted years in Afghanistan*—had brought them to the fight. The Americans would be forced to redeploy.

No country was more vulnerable than tiny Israel, but with the Muslim war to purify the land from the *kafir*—infidel Muslims— perhaps the rise of their enemies was a blessing in disguise. His uncle thought that was the case.

Nicky's orders were to build a network that traded in rumors and arms and to make heads rolls. He was succeeding beyond any reasonable projections. After they finished analyzing the results of this and several other Beta initiatives, then the full-scale implementation of their war plans would begin. His uncle's goal was sixty percent carnage in the Middle East.

Was this actually attainable? Nicky hadn't thought so in the beginning but he was growing more and more confident with each successful mission.

Seventy percent might be more realistic with what we have planned.

Nicky looked at the sheikh. His face was a swollen gourd of wrinkles, but he smiled through the rotten, brownish stumps of teeth, and spat a thick gooey stream of qat in the direction of the American. That was good. Nicky was certain he would live to face another day.

The network is in place. No one knows who is behind it. I will listen to Uncle and delegate what comes next, but far away from the killing zone.

3

Bentonville, Arkansas

JONATHAN ALEXANDER ADJUSTED HIS SILK tie and smoothed back his silver white hair out of years of habit. Both were already perfectly in place. The twin Rolls Royce engines of the Gulfstream G650 lowered in pitch as his private jet began its smooth descent to a small private airfield in Northwest Arkansas.

Even with a soft global economy that hampered the sales of luxury items, the Gulfstream was on backorder for almost five years. The fastest private plane available at 610-miles-per-hour, with an international range of seven thousand miles, he had to have it immediately.

At seventy-three years of age and number eleven on the Forbes List of World Billionaires with a net worth estimated at just over fifty billion—Alexander smiled at the estimate—what was the point in waiting? He doubled the $65 million price tag to take delivery of a model intended for a Russian oil baron who was experiencing a temporary cash flow crisis. The drop in the price of a barrel of crude oil and the enormous cost of expanding a private army to protect oneself from emboldened enemies took a bite from his capital. Alexander knew firsthand the cost of mercenaries.

The Gulfstream wasn't his most expensive or spacious jet, but it had a strategic advantage. Having bought it in the secondary market through a distant company he owned, it was not yet known by friends and enemies that he was the passenger. Anonymous travel was one of the most difficult tasks for a man of his stature and reputation.

Whenever he traveled anonymously, he took extra precautions, including sending his doppelgänger—the Frenchman bore an incredible resemblance to Alexander—to one of his island properties on the big jet, a beautiful woman or two at his side. Alexander paid the man handsomely but suspected he would volunteer for his assignments without remuneration.

Still, every time he flew this route in the Gulfstream he was taking the risk of discovery. Only one man in Northwest Arkansas knew his identity—and despite trusting no one, Alexander trusted him.

It was a crisp late October morning. Alexander's cashmere camel sport jacket would provide him plenty of protection from the chill. He planned to be back in the air within five or six hours. He told Pauline, his most recent traveling companion, she could shop and do her daily ten-kilometer run—the latter was such a strange obsession—but she was to be back at the jet no later than three p.m. They would eat dinner at Per Se in Midtown and then spend the night at his townhome on the Upper East Side off Park Avenue.

He could hear the shower in the stateroom turn off. He wasn't happy that Pauline would not be presentable to see him off, a courtesy that was expected in her role—and it was never good to let hired help think that anything less than excellence was acceptable—but he waved off his irritation for the moment. He had a more important matter on his mind.

Alexander's long time pilot dropped the craft into a soft and perfect three-point landing on the runway of the Louise M. Thaden Field of the Bentonville Municipal Airport. Normally they would land at the Northwest Arkansas Airport, but he preferred to be even more cautious and discrete this trip.

The Gulfstream taxied to a pair of waiting gleaming black Range Rovers and the stairs were quickly lowered.

"Darling, I'll be just a second if you can wait," Pauline called from behind the closed door. "I want to see you off."

He ignored her.

"Jonathan?"

He paused, irritated again.

"Jonathan darling?"

He put on sunglasses and a fedora, and then stepped through the door into the streaming sunshine.

Pauline had been quite excited about finally being included on a long flight in the Gulfstream. Too bad it will be her last trip with me, he thought. She's beautiful; a remarkable beauty that stirred bittersweet memories of distant time in his past. She is intelligent. She is charming. But she's sloppy. You can take the girl out of Belgium, he thought, but you can't take Belgium out of the girl.

He would have Klaus, his personal secretary, work with his lawyers to execute their separation agreement. He wondered if she was bright enough to realize how little she was walking away with when she got a tidy little check for a hundred thousand euros. Not bad for a young person just starting out in life. But the sum paled in comparison to the opulent lifestyle she was experiencing by his side. Her modest payout wouldn't book her two trips on a chartered Gulfstream. He doubted she would have any of the money left by years' end. Young people had little sense of delayed gratification. They wanted things now. No matter. He liked her but wouldn't miss her. Not for long. There were more Paulines out there.

"As is always the case, the flight was a work of art. Such a fine landing, Erich," he said to the ramrod straight captain who tipped his hat to him.

"Thank you, sir. You are kind, sir."

Erich understood the rules of engagement. Erich was always excellent. Too bad for Pauline.

The tall, trim, elegant man exited the plane slowly but gracefully, following his bodyguard, Jules, invisible during the flight, but a force of nature in light of day, to the bottom of the stairs and waited.

Jules opened the back door of the Range Rover and did a thorough physical and electronic search. He repeated the process in the front seat. He then nodded curtly to the driver to pop open the trunk. Jules searched the compartment thoroughly, shut the lid, and next opened a telescopic rod with a mirror to check the undercarriage. The driver looked sullen, though he had been told by the boss that this was standard operating procedure for today's client.

Who does this guy think he is?

As Jules moved back to the front of the car the man asked from the driver's seat he was glued to—instructions had been given that he stay in the car the whole time—"Is this really necessary?"

The last word nearly caught in his throat as he looked up and made eye contact with Jules for the first time.

Jules fixed him with the brightest emerald green eyes the man had ever seen. Looking into Jules piercing stare he wasn't sure he had actually seen green eyes in his entire life. Not like these. What the driver sensed from the blond ape was a calm, dispassionate, almost gentle, hostility. The man was a killer. As a Viet Nam vet who had known his share of men who lived for violence, he was certain of it.

No words were exchanged. Jules continued his detailed inspection. Satisfied, Jules nodded to the chauffeur who silently started the engine. Jules opened the door for Alexander.

I guess us local yokels aren't good enough to open this guy's door.

Jules walked around to the other side of the car but instead of getting in the back, opened the front passenger door, pushed a leather scheduler to the middle, and settled in. His eyes would not leave the driver for the rest of the trip.

Alexander watched and smiled. Jules truly was an artist with intimidation.

A matching SUV awaited Pauline's bidding. He looked back as they pulled away. She still hadn't emerged from the plane.

"I want to see you off, darling." My dear Pauline, you did not take care of business. I must bid you a fond adieu.

She was different than other service companions Alexander had employed through the years. She played the part of devoted mistress well, almost to a tee. But her serene smile and calm disposition couldn't hide the fact that the waters of her soul ran deep. She could pretend to be owned, but not well enough to disguise that it was pretense. She had her own agenda. He liked that.

Sometimes.

4

New York City

"DO WE KNOW ANYTHING YET? What is our friend up to?" Emmanuel Heller asked as he slathered butter and a large dollop of caviar on a slice of freshly-baked sourdough bread.

"We still know nothing. But that might change soon," answered Walter Wannegrin, who just shook his head in amusement as Heller put the knife in his mouth and pulled it out slowly to make sure he devoured every last morsel of the insanely expensive Russian black roe.

"Good! My boss is nervous. More importantly his boss is nervous. Usually I'd just ignore both of them, but frankly, I'm nervous, too."

"That makes you smart, Manny. I keep hearing little tidbits from my sources that should make *all* of us nervous."

"So Wally, you're sure you've found a way inside his defenses?"

No one dared called Walter Wannegrin, Wally—or Emmanuel Heller, Manny—but the two septuagenarians had a friendship that spanned more than sixty years, which afforded the privilege of an intimate casualness.

"I don't *think* I've found a way in, Manny. I *know* I've found a way in. I'm already inside. I have been for five months."

"You could have told me that, Wally," said Heller, dabbing at the corner of a frown with his napkin.

"Manny, you're the one who taught me that once someone knows your secret, it isn't a secret anymore."

"I agree, Wally. But that only applies to everyone in your life but me. I need to know everything," Emmanuel explained as he went into a coughing fit.

His rolls of blubber undulated in time with his distressed hacks and wheezes. Concerned, Walter, thin and nimble, stood, went to his friend, and began slapping him in the middle of his massive back.

"I'm fine, I'm fine," Emmanuel said. "Are you trying to kill me just because I remind you that I must know all secrets?"

"You don't look fine Manny. And I knew you would say that about secrets not applying to you because I know how impatient you are. This is a project that requires patience."

"I've suffered the affliction of patience for a full nine months since we first spoke of the matter. Long enough to have a baby. If you've been inside his gates for five months why don't we know anything yet?"

"You see, I told you. You are too impatient, Emmanuel. This is delicate. We want to find out what he's up to without him knowing we were ever there. Your instructions exactly. You would have us hit the hornet's nest like it was a piñata. In fact, as I recall, that is what you did when we were little boys."

"I think your memory is fuzzy and it was actually you who did that," Manny laughed. "You were older so you made sure I got blamed for it."

"Older by two months, Manny—you could stand up for yourself just fine."

"No Wally, I'm certain it was you. Sixty-one years later I remember that little escapade of yours like it was yesterday."

"Sixty-one years? We are getting old, Manny. Too old to argue about what we both know to be true—you hit the hornet's nest—and for what we're trying to accomplish. I've always looked forward to dying peacefully in my sleep, preferably without a bullet hole in my head."

"We may be old, but that's why we've got to do this. You know as well as I do, actually better since you are a father and I am not, we cannot trust the young ones with something this big. They have too many personal issues from not being breast-fed properly or getting punched in the nose on the playground or some other nonsense someone put in their heads. They get distracted from what is important. That's why I came to you, Walter."

"Exactly. *You* came to me. Now just relax and be patient. Let this operation unfold. No prying. You asked me to do something you can't do yourself. Leave me in peace to do it."

"I must admit, I'm impressed, Walter. You got inside. I wasn't sure that was possible. But five months ago. *Oyez!* What has taken so long to get any information—and what has changed now?"

"You're prying."

"I need a morsel for my masters."

Wannegrin sighed and spoke slowly, "My contractor tells me an opportunity for the acquisition of closely-held personal data has finally presented itself to his agent."

"Soon?"

"Even as we speak. Today or tonight. Maybe right now."

"The man has done little to no meaningful business by computer or a cell phone or land line for years, even though he has the best encryption in the world. Where has Alexander kept the data hidden?"

"You asked me to help and I have done so at considerable expense and danger. And with no exposure to you and your government I would add. Now you want to interrogate me like a juvenile delinquent? You asked for a morsel and against my better judgment, knowing what an appetite you have, I offered you one."

"I am sorry, Walter. You are right. I'm impatient. And when I'm impatient I get rude. Forgive me Wally."

"Impatience. That is exactly why you are always rude, Emanuel. But I love you anyway and you are always forgiven even before you commit one of your many sins. Now it's time for you to get out of my hair and let me finish what you asked me to do. We will know something soon. Maybe a little. Maybe a lot. Time will tell."

"Time we might not have, Wally."

"Time is God's way of keeping everything from happening at the same time, Manny. Just try to have a little patience."

"Wally, I hope you know how grateful I am for your work. That's why I'm taking you to dinner tomorrow night at the Madison Club."

"Yeah, yeah, I know how grateful you are. And I know I should be honored that the legendary Emanuel Heller, the man even presidents of the United States fear, would stop by for a surprise breakfast and then invite me to dinner. But I also know you'll make me pick up the bill."

"Walter, your expense account is better than mine. Much better. We'll both enjoy a much better dinner if you pay."

"That's what you've been telling me all these years."

"We'll drink a toast to many more. The world needs us Wally, even if we are old men."

"I have no argument there, Emmanuel. The world still does need a few old washed up curmudgeons like us, whether or not it knows it. We will lift a glass to celebrate our grand achievement of still being alive. Tomorrow night. At the Madison Club."

The rotund Emanuel Heller pushed his chair back and began the incredible effort it took for him to lift his four hundred pounds from a chair with a grunt and a profanity.

Walter Wannegrin reached over and put a hand on his forearm to stop him. Emanuel settled his bulk back in the cushion gratefully. He looked up at his friend.

"Before you leave Manny, I am curious."

"Aren't we all?"

"Tomorrow night's dinner has been scheduled for more than a month. Why the charade? It's just the two of us. You left your bodyguard in the car. And as security conscious and paranoid as you are to keep your whereabouts and meetings a secret, why did you stop by for breakfast?"

"I was in New York and I was hungry. I knew you were my only sure bet to have a tin of Russian Osetra black caviar to go with bagels and cream cheese."

"I had no bagels and cream cheese. You had to settle for fresh-baked sourdough and Irish butter."

"A small concession when set next to spending time with my best friend and his delicious caviar."

"When aren't you hungry Emanuel? I'm not sure I even tasted the caviar myself. Someone ate an entire twelve-hundred-dollar tin by himself."

"I forget myself when I eat."

"You do. And you change the subject when you don't want to answer a question. Why did you really stop by?"

"The answer is not so sinister, Walter. As I said, the powers that be are nervous and I have to feed them something. Even with a legend they want to know what you've done for them lately."

"Tell them we're inside and poised to make a move."

"I already did. A couple months ago."

"So you lied."

"How can it be a lie when I was right? I was just expressing confidence in my lifelong friend."

"As you should. So remind them you are a legend."

"There is a new Pharaoh in town who knows not Joseph."

"Tell the president to be patient."

"I will. At lunch today. A little birdy tells me that the POTUS plans to turn up the heat on the grill when he questions me. That should dispel any mystery surrounding my visit this morning." Heller looked at his watch. "That's only an hour from now. And I believe I've worked up an appetite."

Wannegrin laughed. "Just tell him to be patient."

"Easier to tell the sun to sleep in for a day, my faithful friend."

"The sun did not rise for Joshua when he defeated the Amorites—perhaps it will not rise for Emmanuel Heller when he strides into his next battle."

"I will receive that as a blessing," Heller said with a smile and nod as he laboriously stood and turned from the exquisite view of Manhattan Island from the 87th floor of Wannegrin's condo in One57.

I wonder if it's true that Wally paid $60 million for this, Heller wondered.

SIXTY-ONE YEARS OF FRIENDSHIP, Wannegrin thought, feeling his own mortality. He remembered the first time he set eyes on Manny, a fat little kid from Brooklyn. Emmanuel's parents had sent him to spend a summer on Walter's family's defiant little kibbutz in Palestine. They wanted to toughen Emmanuel up.

Despite his thick spectacles, his aversion to manual labor, his obesity, his bookish ways, they need never have worried. Emmanuel Heller was one of the toughest men he knew. Give the man a stick and a swarming hornet's nest, and he was fearless.

Emmanuel was the one who broke open the hornet's nest with a stick.

5

Los Angeles, California

FAHAD. THE LEOPARD. HE WAS twenty-five years old. Born on Coney Island Avenue in Brooklyn, New York, his Pakistani parents moved to Culver City, just off the 405, when he was nine-years old, to open a restaurant. His tenth birthday party was at the Wonder World Amusement Park in Anaheim, which was to that point, the greatest day of his life.

But there comes a moment in every young man's life when he must grow up and look at life beyond children's games.

He tightened the wires on the timing mechanism that sat in the top of his toolbox.

It took him two years at Los Angeles Trade Tech, after high school, to get his degree in electrical construction and maintenance. He spent the next two years freelancing for various contractors before being hired on the support staff at Wonder World, with full benefits and a decent hourly wage.

He lifted out the timer and looked again at thousands of nails and metal scraps, which rested on a reservoir filled with three gallons of a highly flammable cocktail, including acetone and gasoline, two easy-to-access Class I flammables. When the clock hit 00:00 a flash of fire would ignite the fuel and propel metal missiles into human flesh, maiming and killing hundreds if not thousands. How many? Zoraiz told him to not worry about details. However many infidel lives he took would be enough to remind the soft, sensual West that their sins would not go unpunished.

Almost sixty thousand visitors would be at Wonder World on Friday night. Most would stay for the fireworks show at ten o'clock. His shift ended at eight p.m. That would give him an hour to place his tool chest in a small garden next to the square of the Enchanted Palace, the area where close to ten thousand people would watch an array of sizzling, dizzying lights explode overhead. It was the most popular and crowded spot in the park at that time. He would open the lid, set the clock, cover it with a thin fabric camouflage, and walk calmly to the employee exit. He would be in his car and on the 405 when the real fireworks started.

He thought of Zoraiz. He met him at mosque when he was eighteen. Zoraiz was the man who helped him understand who he was as a Muslim in an infidel land. He taught him the Koran and how to be a man. A real man.

If Zoraiz had asked him to sacrifice his own life, Fahad would have done so willingly and without question. Zoraiz had helped him see that life is much bigger and grander than earthly existence.

His parents wanted to know why he hadn't started a family of his own.

Perhaps now he would. But first he would have to get a new job.

He closed the lid on the toolbox and took a few steps back. It looked perfect. Just like a toolbox.

6

New York City

BURKE WAS TOWEL DRYING HIS hair in a cramped bathroom on the fifteenth floor of a nondescript hotel in the Hell's Kitchen neighborhood of Manhattan when his phone chirped.

He had cranked out three hundred push ups in sets of fifty with one-minute recovery breaks thirty minutes ago. He had to take the call. Thirty minutes ago he wouldn't have been able to speak.

"Yes?"

"Any word?" The voice was mechanical. Whoever his contractor was used an electronic voice scrambler.

"You'll know when I know."

"No problems?"

"You'll know that, too. But only when I do."

"I like to be kept informed."

"You have been and you will be. But we both agreed to limit unnecessary contact."

"With what I'm paying you, *I* get to define unnecessary."

If the man was in the same room with him right now, Burke wasn't sure he would be able to restrain himself from inflicting serious bodily damage—even if his own nakedness made him feel very vulnerable. The problem was he didn't know who the man was. He often didn't know his clients' identity and they really didn't know who he was either. Better for both parties. But this project was different. A gnawing in the pit of his stomach told him he should have spent more time figuring out who hired him. In the early days of his business, he always did. But even a seared conscience struggles with the nature of work requested of him by some of his best customers, so over time Burke took a "don't ask, don't tell" approach to knowing who paid his light bills.

The parameters for his current assignment were insanely impossible. Stealing from a man like Jonathan Alexander, without him being the wiser, was chiseling away at Burke's usual calm and indifferent manner.

When Burke informed his client that the final stage of the operation was green lighted, the barrage of calls started out as a nuisance. Now he wondered if there was another reason. The man and whoever he worked for was up to something. Burke knew betrayal—a devastating betrayal—that still haunted his every waking moment. That kept his paranoia finely tuned. Was his client trying to pinpoint his exact location? He pulled the phone from his ear and looked at the screen of his prepaid out-of-date Nokia with deep suspicion. No doubt. He could smell betrayal in the air.

"I'll be in touch soon," Burke said.

"The sooner the better."

He pulled up his undershorts, followed by a pair of jeans. He wrestled his arms and head into a soft wool sweater. He tugged up his Swiftwick compression socks and tightened the laces on a pair of lightweight Asics running shoes. He didn't sense imminent action, but always better to be prepared for fight or flight than surprised by what might be waiting for you outside your door or on the street.

Burke rarely spent time in New York City anymore. Too crowded. Too busy. Too self-important. But he needed to stick around for the return of his contractor who was in way over her head with such a dangerous prey. Despite the directive to not let Alexander know anyone had been snooping in his business, this was where Burke planned to extract his operative. He would snatch Pauline tonight. That thought solidified in his mind. Something his client wouldn't like but wouldn't know was coming until it happened. He could argue later that the risk of keeping her in Alexander's presence was a greater risk.

Burke looked at the phone again. He slid the back panel off and tossed the battery in the waist basket. Something was in the air. He packed his few belongings quickly, forcing his breathing to remain even. He then worked through the room quickly to wipe away prints and any traces he had been there. Anything in the trash went with him to be deposited in random dumpsters outside a radius of at least one mile. Time to change to a new untraceable phone and location.

The problem was, as he well knew, nothing and nobody was untraceable.

7

Turin, Italy

WHEN AC MILAN VISITED TURIN to square off against Juventus
in a Lega Serie A football showdown, all 41,475 seats were sure to be
filled, sometimes with more than one person to a seat. The two teams
were in a tight battle to be crowned *Campione d'Italia* and for a spot in
the UEFA Euro Cup Championship.

With a 1-1 tie at the 85th minute mark, and the black and white
striped "jailhouse" uniforms of Juventus setting up to take a corner
kick, the stadium vibrated from the sound of thousands of raucous
voices screaming encouragement to Filippo Esposito, a homegrown
hero, as he bent over to place and replace the position of the ball in
order for him execute a perfect crossing strike.

No one noticed two men standing on the causeway above the top
row, 49 meters from the pitch. Their heads were drawn close as they
would point to various entrance and egress points for fans and then
heatedly discuss a point of contention.

Esposito struck the ball on the right inseam of his boot, hooking a
screamer around the mouth of the goal, where the ball met the forehead
of his teammate perfectly, caroming back across the goal set where it
cleared the side and cross bars, mere centimeters to spare, nestling into
the back corner of the net.

More than 41,000 sets of eyes followed as Esposito sprinted across the field, shedding his jersey en route, to join his teammates in a corner celebratory scrum.

The two men were still talking closely as they descended the exit ramps, ignoring the roar of the crowd shouting, "Fileeepo!"

A member of the Carabinieri, straddling a BMW motorcycle, noticed the two men exiting the stadium early. He smiled. Must be AC Milan fans, he thought. Bad losers, but at least they are not causing trouble.

"I'm not arguing your point," the taller man hissed at his companion. "Yes. Of course. The stadium is best."

"And the discothèques have been hit so many times, they get no reaction," the shorter man interrupted.

"Yes! Agreed! But this is only phase one. We aren't ready to hit the stadium. That can come next. What we must do is succeed. Better a thousand at a disco than failing to set up correctly at a football stadium and killing no one. Do you think we will be entrusted with a second chance?"

The shorter man scowled and said, "small vision, small courage, and small faith produce small outcomes."

"True," the taller man responded conciliatorily, knowing he had won the argument. "But when we are faithful in small tasks, we will be entrusted with larger tasks in the days ahead. You shall have your football stadium in the near future."

The two men exchanged kisses on each cheek before parting at the entrance of the Torino Porta Nuova railway station. The taller man was taking a train to Milan and the shorter man a train to Rome.

The taller man shook his head slowly from side-to-side as he walked down the open air concourse. His compatriot, like so many other young men, was too impatient. He was willing to screw up an important attack—probably blowing his foot off during the setup—rather than go for a sure victory and learn. We've not handled the explosive required to implode the Stadium. Better to wait until we are ready.

I would actually like to see if AC Milan can still win it all this year, the taller man, a die-hard Devil fan, thought with a smile, approaching his platform at a brisk pace.

8

Bentonville, Arkansas

AS JONATHAN ALEXANDER DROVE OFF in the first Range Rover, Pauline looked out the side window one more time to make sure Jonathan and Jules were gone. Her heart was hammering a staccato pattern that made her feel faint. It was time to finish what she was hired to do.

I have to get out of here.

PRETTY COUNTRYSIDE, JONATHAN ALEXANDER THOUGHT as he peered out the window on the country drive. Not like the countryside surrounding his residence in Switzerland, but charming in its own way.

Twenty-five minutes later the car pulled into the parking lot of a low-slung, rectangular brick structure. A concrete-floored, open pavilion with a painted metal roof covering long rows of picnic tables was off to one side. The parking lot was pitted and broken asphalt with splashes of green where weeds had fought their way to the surface to breach their prison ceiling. The building's only defining feature was a cross. It looked to be fashioned from construction

I-beams, anchored in small plot of grass surrounded by a foot-high stone fringe.

Pretty countryside but the architecture leaves something to be desired.

A youngish man—Alexander didn't know his exact age, but assumed late thirties or early forties—wearing a cheap suit and scuffed shoes was waiting for him at the front door, per his instructions. This would be their first and only meeting at the man's workplace.

He really should bulldoze this ugly little building and erect something more edifying to the spirit. But after today, regretfully, that will no longer be within his purview.

Alexander frowned. This is the man I've flown thousands of miles to meet with on numerous occasions—always the same stateroom at the Hyatt Regency in Fayetteville, both of us ascending via the service elevator, of course. This is my spiritual mentor, the man whose blessing I seek yet again. This puzzled Alexander. What was the pull? History is filled with stranger convergences and meetings, he thought. He almost smiled.

Alexander gently rubbed two fingertips above his right ear, feeling the familiar groove from an old battle scar earned when his last name was Alexopolous. That was a long time ago and a different life. He ran his palm over the spot again carefully, slowly, and almost lovingly. He liked to tell himself he did it to make sure the jagged disfigurement was properly hidden by the feathering of his elegantly coiffed, slightly longish hair. But the truth was that touching it brought him a sense of comfort. He was a survivor. It reminded him of who he was and where he came from. What it had taken to get where he was.

Maybe there is a God and he brought me here, Alexander thought, his hand outstretched in greeting. Or more likely, the thorn in God's flesh brought me here. Or maybe it was just Google.

Blame it on a bout of insomnia a few years back. Sleep had been so hard to come by that he broke his strict protocol of no more than a few hours of television a week and started late night channel surfing.

He stopped to listen to an American minister with a hard-to-understand southern twang preach on Armageddon, the End Times, the Last Days, and other things Alexander wasn't sure he ever heard about in the occasional Greek Orthodox training he received in his childhood. When the preacher spoke of the Apostle John writing the Book of Revelation from the Island of Patmos, Alexander felt a tingling. His father was from Patmos. They had fished the waters around the island and hiked the rocky, desolate hills when he was a little boy.

Several times Alexander tried to click the button on the remote but something arrested him. It was one of the rare moments when he felt such a mysterious tug at his heart from a religious source. He felt Marx got one thing almost right: *religion is the opiate of the masses.* That was a good thing so he kept a healthy respect for most religious traditions for those times when he needed to use them as a tool to further his business interests. He contributed to the full range of faiths, whether he liked them or not. The only checks that he didn't like to write were to Islamic causes. Islam is not really an opiate, he thought; it is definitely a stimulant. But business needed oil so he did what was expected to court the princes and mullahs.

That will change soon.

Alexander listened raptly to the enthusiastic and animated descriptions of the one world government, the Battle of Armageddon, the mark, the Beast … it was … it was magnificent. Better by far than the vision presented by men in secret meetings who thought they still controlled the puppet strings of human history.

History is no longer under the command of a few enlightened men.

The biblical version of the Apocalypse. Did he believe it? Not at the time. Not now; at least not literally. But he knew others believed every word and sentence wholeheartedly. A seed of thought began to emerge on how such knowledge could empower plans that were already under way.

After hearing the sermon, he invited a professor from Princeton Theological Seminary to dinner at his Manhattan townhome to learn more. The man gave him a two-hour lecture on the sociology of religion to explain why some people got such fanciful and outrageous notions of the End Times. The man bored him. He was no help. Alexander decided to forget Patmos and St. John's Revelation and the Beast, but his mind kept circling back, pulled by an invisible, mystical tether.

He next visited a Methodist minister, a well-known religious author and close confidant of New York City's devout Conservative Jewish mayor—maybe this man could cover more theological bases based on his range of contacts—who explained that the Book of Revelation wasn't prophecy but a look back at conditions under the Emperor Nero. He was very knowledgeable about Early Church history. A little more interesting than the professor's lecture, but the talk did not stir his blood. It had no power, no pull. It was not what he wanted to hear nor needed. Alexander determined to let the sleeping dog of End Times rhetoric sleep. But the invisible fetter and his imagination betrayed him yet again.

He met with a Catholic Bishop in Vatican City who explained the use of imagery in the Bible and how it was better to have a more optimistic view of life and the world—"Remember the doxology, 'world without end, Amen, Amen'"—and that Alexander shouldn't be preoccupied with the End Times. When he asked if Alexander wanted to make a confession Alexander almost laughed. He would go to the grave with his secrets and he wasn't a fan of Catholicism anyway. He felt the Catholic Church gave too much support to his Sicilian competitors when he was fighting his way up in the world.

He next spoke with a Baptist evangelist in Houston, Texas, and listened to how people he had never heard of were misinterpreting Scripture on when the rapture would happen and who would face the Tribulation. The man was enthused. But he couldn't stay in a straight line to save his life. He had identified too many false notions that needed to be corrected—none of which Alexander was aware of—which made the discourse rambling and confusing in his ears. It felt like trying to get a sip of water from a fire hose.

Not sure what to do next, Alexander returned to Greece and visited Mount Athos, a small peninsula jutting into the Aegean Sea and home to twenty Eastern Orthodox monasteries under the jurisdiction of the Ecumenical Patriarch of Constantinople. Only men were allowed on the holy ground. Visitors had two ways to prove their gender; either grow a beard or drop their pants before boarding a ferry. Alexander grew a beard. He met with a scholarly priest who taught at the University of Thessaloniki and who was on a sabbatical to study some rare extant Byzantine manuscripts. When Alexander asked the professor about the Beast of Revelation, the man lit up as he explained:

"Though John's Revelation of Jesus Christ is not read in the liturgy, the book is most important to our understanding of being the one true church. It is the Beast who will seek to corrupt the one true faith through unity with heretics. I worry even now when I hear reports of the amount of time our Patriarch spends in Rome."

Alexander listened attentively but lost real interest as he realized that it was an ecclesiastical war the priest described. Ministers are as bad as economists on interpreting what they are looking at, Alexander mused as his barber shaved the last stubble of his beard with a straightedge the next day.

Forget this, Alexander thought. You don't need God's help or blessing. If there truly is a Creator God, the one closest to him, the true son, Lucifer, has already taught us that God's judgment is not always correct nor fair. The Morning Star has also taught us that God can be tricked and even exploited.

Exploiting God. Using God. Was that not the story and pathos of all religions? The thought of manipulating the divine would not let him forget the message he heard on late night TV. It kept him uncharacteristically restless. He still wanted to talk to someone who could explain what was believed—really believed—about the Last Days and especially the Beast.

Alexander didn't know if he was an agnostic or an atheist, so that probably made him the former. But perhaps knowing he was realistically entering the final decade or possibly two of his mortal life—his only life, he assumed—he had developed a ... a what? A Freudian need to create a god, bubbling up from the superego based on having lousy parents and a life filled with unacknowledged guilt? Seemed too dramatic. He had set in motion the planning and research stages of his legacy to the world, but had stopped short of pulling the trigger. Literally pulling the trigger. He felt the need for a touch of the divine—a sign—to serve as a shiny talisman of protection and guidance over the most important and difficult task of his life.

Killing more than five billion people and resetting the clock on the tipping point of whether the earth could continue to house its human inhabitants—the Malthusian Equation—was no small undertaking.

Alexander rationalized that Napoleon Bonaparte consulted with a clairvoyant, Madam Normand, before his great victories. Alexander the Great sought out the Oracle of Delphi before conquering the Persian Empire with the belief he was a god. When she refused to give him audience, he dragged her by the hair from the temple to the town square and beat her until she spoke the words he traveled to hear.

Was that what he was doing to this man?

Hitler had so many superstitions, from the number seven to the magic of the swastika he found in Egyptian symbolism, he had obviously outdone himself and taken the need for a touch of the divine far too far.

But still ... why shouldn't he consult with—and be blessed by— the divine before his conquest? Was that so unreasonable? Achilles' mother, Thetis, had made her warrior son invincible—had it not been for holding him by his heel. Could the Revelation of John help him bathe in River Styx fully?

The ancient Greeks believed that as long as people repeated your name you were immortal. *My conquest of the world's worthless is my path to immortality,* Alexander thought again. *I must do it right. And I must continue to write down the words of my truth so people will know it was me who bestowed the gift. Forever.*

There was another practicality to truly understanding the words of Revelation. If God was real, he might awake from his slumber and choose to oppose Alexander, making him an enemy to Alexander's plan to save the world. That made it even more of an imperative to understand this strange, esoteric book. He needed to know how best to defeat anything God sent against him. Alexander suspected that the outcome of a battle that pitted the forces of heaven against Lucifer's earthly incarnation was not the foregone conclusion the Apostle John made it out to be. But still better to understand as much as possible.

In frustration over not hearing the words, the conviction, the blessing—or cursing—he wanted to hear, Alexander typed into the Google search line on a computer at an internet café in Paris, *Armageddon, the Apocalypse, the Beast, the False Prophet, the Last Days, Revelation, the Island of Patmos, the end of the world.* He thought that might cover everything.

To his amazement, one country preacher, Reverend Dwight Garrison, located outside of Bentonville, Arkansas, right in the heart of Middle America and Walmart country, was preaching on those very topics the coming Sunday. He had been considerate enough to tag all those phrases on his church's online announcement and the Google spiders popped the preacher to the second page of Alexander's search. Alexander was going to have Klaus call the reverend to set up the appointment, but some things were better handled personally. He decided he himself would call to let the man know he needed to meet with him and that he would reward him generously for his time. He told the man he needed some spiritual guidance.

"You don't need to bring any money, but I'm happy to talk to you."

After each meeting, whether by phone or in person at the Hyatt—a foolish risk, truth be told—Alexander gave Garrison the user name and password for a blind account in the Cayman Islands, which grew by one million dollars each time they interacted. It was funded through a shell company that was untraceable to Alexander, but still a potential entanglement that needed to be severed. Garrison still hadn't withdrawn a single dollar. Alexander made sure Garrison knew the account balance. The man now had more than seven million dollars to build a glorious temple to the God he believed in so ardently. Alexander was both impressed and unimpressed by the man's stubborn refusal to use the funds. A couple hundred thousand dollars, just one little withdrawal, would pave the parking lot and build a suitable steeple to draw attention heavenward and away from the ugly low-slung structure that was better suited to serve as a machine shop. Reverend Garrison was a good man but appeared to have a shortage of vision, Alexander mused. Yet here he, the world-famous Jonathan Alexander, was back to meet with his spiritual mentor. He gave Garrison a curt nod as they shook hands.

Once Garrison bestowed the blessing of his understanding—a deadly blessing that both killed and gave life to the world—he, Garrison, would be dead. Even if the funds were untraceable to him, it was actually better Garrison hadn't withdrawn any of the money. There would be no walking the cat back to Alexander once the account was closed. Garrison's death would be unfortunate but necessary.

"Welcome back Mr. Alexander."

"Thank you Reverend Garrison." He paused by the battered front door. "You know you could build something completely new with the donations I have gifted you and your ministry."

Garrison looked over his shoulder at the structure and said, "It's not fancy, but this is something my people and I have built with our own means and giving. We're pretty proud of it. If we built from what you gave, it might not feel like we were trusting God to provide."

"But feelings can't always be trusted, Reverend Garrison. I believe it was you who told me that. Perhaps God is indeed providing for you through me. You've said such things yourself. I recall a humorous story you told me about a drowning man being offered a row boat and, I believe, a helicopter as well, both of which he refused."

"Your point is well taken, Mr. Alexander, but I just haven't found peace on taking your money. Believe me I've prayed and will keep praying."

"When you do feel peace, I cannot wait to see what you build," Alexander said, thinking again that Garrison's refusal to access the account would make things simpler.

Actually this would be the last time he planned for the two of them to meet in person or otherwise. He had just a few final questions left to ask. One of them was already embedded within the question of how God provides. Could it be that if God actually existed, he might have been waiting for such a man as Alexander to begin a great purge to cleanse the world? Was he the helicopter sent to save a dying world from the swirling waters of brutality and ignorance?

"It's mighty tempting to wire a check to the Wells Fargo Bank just to see the expression on the teller's face when I ask her to confirm that a million dollars has been deposited in the church account."

"Only one million?"

Garrison reddened and mustered a forced laugh.

The man's earnestness was truly inspiring. He was the right man to bestow the blessing.

"If you have a change of heart, if you find your peace, please tell me if her expression measures up to your picture of it," Alexander said.

Garrison just shrugged awkwardly. He actually looked a little embarrassed. He had been praying about the money, Alexander thought.

Alexander looked at the ugly brick rectangle. As he drove for his first visit to where the man pastored a small flock of believers, he had pictured a charming white clapboard country church set on a rise with stately trees as backdrop. No matter. He liked the man. He always felt a rare peace after meeting with Garrison. He really didn't expect Garrison to be able to answer his questions. Garrison still didn't seem to grasp the questions behind his questions.

He is much too earnest for his own good.

Garrison was no Oracle of Delphi. He would not make Alexander drag him to the town square for a beating before bestowing his blessing.

"Let's go on inside, sir. We can meet in my office."

As Alexander stepped over the threshold, he reached into the breast pocket of his cashmere jacket and froze.

9

The Isle of Patmos

ALMOST SHOW TIME FOR MARIAMA. At least the curtain for Act I was about to be drawn back. Dr. Claire Stevens looked at the azure sky and black rippling waters of the Aegean Sea as she went through the thought process of their target location one more time.

Sana'a, Yemen, according to legend was founded by Shem, one of Noah's sons. Along with Jericho and Damascus, it was one of the three oldest continuously inhabited cities in the world, people having called it home for at least 2,500 years if archeologists and historians could be believed. The Prophet Mohammed visited the land now known as Yemen. Great Imams taught there. Architectural evidence proved that Solomon's lover, the Queen of Sheba, was from the land. She was important to Muslims even if she lived more than one thousand years before the rise of Islam—and even if she was a woman.

Was Sana'a a major power center? No. But it was symbolically important. That was a good start. Fomenting religious fervor and violence was a major part of the planning.

But violence was unpredictable if you wanted to kill people—millions—no billions—of people. More was needed and she was certain Mariama would do her deadly work well.

Most of the twenty-three million Yemenis were Arab, but originally it was a Semitic culture—and once a nominally Christian nation under Ethiopian rule. The roots of Islamic Yemen were tied to the Zaydi Order of Shia Islam, founded by the Twelfth Great Imam, Al al-Hadi in the 9th Century. A small majority of Yemenis belonged to the Shafi'I order of Sunni Islam.

For nearly three decades, Yemen was the only democratic republic on the Arabian Peninsula; all other nations were kingdoms or emirates. What was Yemen now? Hard to tell. After the coup by the Ansar Allah—"supporters of Allah"—there was the political chaos created by two seats of government. Yemen had a long history of civil war and would again, she was sure. Sooner than later.

If there really was a God, why would he need supporters? Jews. Christians. Muslims. Buddhists. They all make the same ontological mistake of turning wish into reality.

Yemeni law and the official stance of the Islamic Clergy still guaranteed religious freedom, which accounted for the 3,500 Christians, 40 Hindu, and 500 indigenous Jews that lived and worshipped there, and which was often cited as proof of the nation's religious tolerance. Claire laughed and shook her head at the irony. Forty Hindu? Why had they stayed? It was just the type of nuanced ridiculousness her parents would lap up as they railed against the notion of God. That religious freedom, however, did not extend to proselytizing Muslims— nor allowing Muslims to convert.

Freedom is a fluid concept.

The unemployment rate in Yemen was 35 percent. The illiteracy rate was nearly 60 percent. It wasn't hard to figure out why. Only seven books were published in the country each year, all dealing with Islam.

Seven books? Really?

With a divided government putting the country on the verge of a new civil war, historical grievances between the north and south, and unemployment comes unrest and the growth of a radicalism that was already rooted in the nation's psyche. Yemen was a fascinating mix of progressive and conservative Islamic thought. It was one of the reasons that Jordan had been eliminated from consideration for the Mariama beta. That country was just too moderate—the radicals they needed to mobilize would probably applaud anything that happened to King Abdullah and his country.

The fact that Yemen bordered Saudi Arabia made it strategically essential to disrupting the wealthy but sleepy peninsula.

Claire argued for releasing a kiss from Mariama in the Al Saleh Mosque in Sana'a. It was Yemen's largest and most modern mosque. Forty-five thousand men could gather in the 220 thousand square foot hall, with room for almost 2,000 women in the upstairs gallery—another proof of their moderate nature, in this case, for how they treated women. Claire snorted. Dedicated in 2008, Al Saleh was located in the southern outskirts of a city with more than one hundred mosques. It was named for the nation's first elected president. The Yemen government—or more accurately governments—ostensibly tolerated no religiously motivated violence, but it was well known that the Al Saleh Mosque, despite being a major tourist attraction, despite being in the center of a country where even Sunnis worked hard to curtail Sunni and Shia radicalism, was a center for Al-Qaeda recruiting, training, and planning.

That made it too big and too obvious for the beta test.

That wasn't her opinion. But she lost the argument. Her face burned at the thought of the man who had recruited her speaking to her as if she was a child.

"Just trust those of us with a little more experience in the Middle East than you," Dr. Rodger Patton said to assuage her hurt feelings. His condescension had the opposite effect.

Just trust you? Not likely.

Patton was a paternalistic prick ... even if he was right in this instance. The group consensus was the mosque was too young to be beloved and too radical to be perceived as innocent. The goal of the beta test, she was pointedly reminded, wasn't the amount of immediate carnage but achieving something noticeable enough to gauge efficacy— and just as importantly to measure the response generated. It was hoped what they were doing would induce a strong response, a violent response.

They still don't believe Mariama will accomplish more than their guns and bombs. Let's see if they feel that way when she is introduced in Beijing and Moscow and Mexico City and Buenos Aires. She'll make traditional mass warfare a quaint obsolescence.

So Claire had gone back to the drawing board and presented the Great Mosque in the Old City, home of the oldest extant copies of the Quran. The ancient mosque was built in 634 A.D. by most accounts. Some claimed it was planned and ordered by the Prophet himself. Some claimed it was pre-Islamic and built by the Byzantines, first as a pagan Roman temple and then a Catholic cathedral. Some claimed it was largely a work from the 8th Century Abbasid period. What no one disputed was that it was the center of religious life in Yemen, characterized as devout but not radical. Not radical being relative, of course.

Like the city itself, the mosque was burned into the consciousness and identity of Muslims in all forms and locations.

The group was right.

I get it. I agree. Just don't talk to me like I'm a child.

That made the Great Mosque the perfect choice. The response to the beta would ostensibly be much more powerful than the provocation itself. That was if the others were underestimating Mariama's raw efficacy to kill.

I believe they are.

Dr. Claire Stevens shivered as the night breeze ruffled and lifted the edges of her nightdress. She slid the door behind her as she went inside her apartment. She wondered if Nicky was well or even alive. The man wore the souvenirs of his work on his body.

She hoped everyone else was doing their job as well as she was.

Mariama, I could not save you. But I will make sure your name lives forever.

10

Northern Yemen

MALMAK NODDED TO YUSUF. YUSUF wedged the claw of the crowbar beneath the lid of the crate and pried it loose a couple inches. He repeated the process at various intervals and then popped the top off.

Malmak's eyes gleamed. Surely the Prophet was gracious to hear his prayers. How else could this abundant gift be his?

Sheikh Malmak led a proud but poor tribe based in the Saudi Arabia city of Tarim on the border with Yemen. Most of his tribe lived in the northern hills of Yemen. With these weapons he would finally become a player, not a spectator; an initiator, not a reactor. He would now be remembered not only as a man of pure words, but also as a man of mighty deeds. He would fulfill the destiny of his exalted name.

Hours earlier Malmak had ordered the death of Sulaymon Ibn Abd Allah's son. But what could the man do about it? His hold on power was long overdue to crash and burn. He pompously had appropriated the name of a great historical leader who had fought to restore the tenets of true Islam, who had fought to destroy the corruption of the infidels, and who had struck terror and death into the heart of Christendom. Sulaymon was not fit for such a glorious name. He had compromised too freely. He must pay the price for the spiritual drift that infected so many of his subjects. His son's death was an earnest payment.

The exercise continued for hours. Each crate contained new delights. Lightweight Kalashnikov AK-47 rifles, RPG mortar launchers, and the ammunition to give teeth to the brand new assault jeeps, troop transports, and hybrid tanks that had already been delivered.

The Greek had delivered everything he promised, including a Russian military veteran of the Chechen wars—an enemy of Allah—something he would have to overlook until the man was of no further use—to train his young warriors.

The Greek had also saved him from the disaster of losing Allah's gift to Sulaymon and his tribe of compromisers and collaborators with the enemies of Allah. He now had the means to do more than cut off the head of the sheikh's beloved son.

Malmak was a man of history. Full retribution for the Wahhabi invasion of Tarim two centuries earlier would come to full fruition now. The Wahhabi's had slaughtered and burned the city of his fathers. To add insult to inglorious injury, they had redrawn the border to split his tribe between two countries, insuring their slow, steady, inglorious decline.

Malmak spat a thick stream of qat.

Death to those who destroyed the writings of true Islam and death to those who forget such crimes against the faithful.

11

Devil's Den Hiking Trail, Ozark National Forest

THE FOREST WAS PAULINE'S CATHEDRAL. She winded through gloomy arbors, an occasional burst of light piercing and caressing her troubled soul on the path.

I don't ever want to stop. Can I run until everything that has been done to me, everything I've done, is behind me?

Everything Pauline had done the past six months had been a tortured and harrowing lie, except for what she was about to do now. She had always loved to run. Now she depended on her daily outing as a tenuous strand to sanity. Sleeping with a megalomaniacal billionaire could do that to you, she thought.

She needed to run like she needed air. It reminded her that she was not the person she had become. Someday soon she would become her true self. She would not be a victim of her circumstances forever.

She had reached the moment that would change her life, but she wondered how she had ever got here. She wanted to believe her life would work out, filled with happiness and wealth. But she had believed before to no avail.

Running with long smooth strides, breathing hard but regular, she exhilarated in the rare, exquisite feeling of personal power—no one can touch me here—as she wended up and down the path of a lush forest path that Klaus had found for her.

The second gleaming black Range Rover had brought her to the trailhead at Devil's Den State Park, about an hour south of the airport. The driver would wait for her to circle back to the same beginning spot of the strenuous, fifteen-mile course—she told the driver she would be back in two hours; he figured it would be closer to three—and then take her to a local day spa where she would be pampered and prepped to look stunning for dinner at Per Se on Columbus Circle just south of Central Park. The flight would be less than two hours and she planned to look ravishing—beyond ravishing—which was, she knew, her only defense in the world of Jonathan Alexander and corporate espionage.

The dress she selected magically wove together strands of provocative and revealing with tasteful and refined. Money might not buy everything but it came close.

Maybe she had become the greedy superficial person she was pretending to be.

Pauline wondered again about Burke, the man who hired her to spy on Jonathan Alexander, pretending to be the billionaire's mistress. Actually, there was no pretending when she was with him. She was indeed a highly paid commodity in the service industry.

Burke. Was that his first or last name? Strange time to be wondering that. What had he gotten her into? Who was he? She had spent months of preparation with him, but knew so little about him. He was an American. He was well put together physically. Six-three? Six-four? Maybe 200 pounds of muscle. Good teeth and hair. His deportment indicated he was prosperous, but in a non ostentatious way. No suits made from exotic fabrics, just jeans, a cotton oxford shirt open at the top of the chest, and a navy blue sport jacket.

Was he rich? The money required for expensive logistics were no issue with him. She knew that he was working for someone else, someone else was paying the bills. That someone else might be working for yet another person up the food chain. But Burke was simple. He probably had a fortune squirrelled away.

Pauline felt a pang of sadness as she thought again, Burke was a man I had almost come to believe was a good man. But a good man would not have put her where she was.

The month-long training and briefing with Burke had been simple. Jonathan Alexander had begun to carry a small leather journal in his suit pocket. He had never previously been seen taking or keeping notes. Apparently Alexander had a prodigious memory and plenty of hired help to do something as menial as committing ink to paper. When something changed with a man as powerful as Alexander, even something as simple as starting to ink words on paper, people noticed and got very curious. Getting in on the right side of a Jonathan Alexander deal could make you a fortune or save you from financial disaster.

Whoever was close enough to Alexander to observe the change reported the journal had to be important. It was never separated from the man unless it was locked up. When he returned to his estate near Geneva, the first thing he would do was go to his office and place it in his personal safe. Something big must be in it for him to add an extra layer of security to his already heavily guarded Swiss compound.

How did Burke and whomever he was working for know this? She could only assume that whoever commissioned the assignment had someone reasonably close to the man. Klaus? Impossible to read him. Jules? Not smart enough. He was a jackhammer that bludgeoned Alexander's problems. Nicky? He was blood related to Alexander. She doubted that Burke knew either. But there was obviously a rat in Alexander's pantry.

What did a billionaire write in his journal? That was the question for inquiring minds.

"Maybe he writes gibberish," Burke answered when she raised the question with him. "Maybe he draws cartoons. Maybe he has simply decided he wants to keep a diary. Maybe he is writing a novel."

She wanted to be taken seriously. So when she pouted at his cavalier joking, he said something that still haunted her: "It is quite possible that whatever he commits to the velum is what is most important to him. You don't want to know what is in there. If you get the chance to look, close your eyes. Just take the pictures of the pages and make it appear as if it has never been disturbed. Curiosity killed the cat and I am afraid it will kill you, too. Pauline, do you understand what I am saying?"

She had nodded yes meekly as she looked into his burning eyes.

Truth was she had wanted to get a response from Burke, but that wasn't it.

So whatever it was that Alexander wrote, his friends, enemies, investors, bankers, large companies, and governments desperately wanted to read the words. They wanted to know what was most important to Alexander.

Burke was always professional, but he couldn't hide his attraction for Pauline. He hadn't been able to the night he showed up as her knight in shining armor either. Cynically she suspected he wanted to take her for a test drive before placing her in Alexander's site lines—and bedroom—for the data snatch, but he remained on task. Too bad. How would she have responded if he had tried? She was attracted to him and would love to have seen what might happen. But like a long line of other men, he was using her, even if no sex was involved—at least not with him. And despite a glimmer of hope that once flickered in her heart, how could she think he might be the man of valor and honor she had always longed for? He was sending her on an assignment that required her to sleep with another man.

That had settled what her response would be in her mind. She longed for him to make a romantic move so she could turn him down. She wanted to see a flicker of pain and rejection in his eyes.

Pauline was sure Burke was trying to impress her when he told her that Alexander wrote only with a Fulgor Nocturnus fountain pen made by Tibaldi of Florence. Alexander won it at an auction in China for a reported eight million US dollars.

After Burke's firm and unmistakable response the first time she asked him what he thought was in the journal—*you don't want to know*—Burke ignored any other questions she might raise about what made securing the ink on velum so important. But in their last prep meeting, she thought it was a slip, he told her all of Alexander's email and phone accounts had been hacked for years—and that Alexander was well aware of the fact. This might be the only record of his true thoughts.

He immediately regretted telling her and told her to forget what he said.

"It is not safe for you to know things about Alexander that a woman in your position would not be expected to know. Believe me, Pauline, it will get you killed if something like that slips out in an unguarded moment."

A woman in my position? Thank you, Burke. Please don't forget you put me in this position.

Burke failed to mention that what he told her to do with that tidbit of information was impossible—*how do you forget what you know?*

It wasn't hard to figure out—not even for a beautiful blonde, she smiled—that Alexander's enemies or competitors thought he was on to something big, something major, some new world-changing business opportunity, that could only be discovered in the ink dispensed by an eight-million-dollar pen.

Stealing the notepad would be simple enough. But her job was to photograph every page and return it into Alexander's care, undetected. She was told to take no risks—not a real possibility with the way Alexander lived his life under the watchful eye of Jules—and to take as long as needed—as long as that was within sixth months of her start date. The payout was all or nothing. Succeed and earn two million euros. Fail and get stuck with Alexander's usual consolation prize of a hundred thousand euros when he discarded yet another mistress.

"Maybe he'll marry me," she told Burke defiantly.

"Never happen," Burke responded curtly. "He's married. Even his worst detractors know he is fiercely loyal to his wife."

Huh?

"Don't ask," was all Burke added.

Two million euros or one-hundred-thousand euros. A big difference between the sums, but still hard to lose either way, she thought. A hundred thousand euros was nice, but two million changed everything for the rest of her life.

So when Alexander went into the aircraft bathroom to check his hair she nicked the portfolio from his jacket pocket that lay at the foot of their bed on the Gulfstream. Her heart was hammering so hard as she helped him on with his jacket that she nearly ran to the small bathroom for a shower.

"Don't leave before I'm done darling, I want to see you off," was all she eked out.

The journal was now carefully tucked in her fanny pack. Pauline knew the grains of sand in the hourglass to successfully complete her mission were nearing the end. No way was she going to settle for a consolation prize after living every day wondering if it would be her last within Alexander's fortressed life. She had already determined this was the trip to do the deed and alerted Burke it was make or break time. She had been right. This was the one, singular moment she had access to Jonathan Alexander's Holy Grail—and the promise of two million euros.

She had sex with Alexander most nights, but it was understood she was to return to her own room once finished. He preferred to sleep alone. *Preferred* was not quite an adequate word. *Insisted* was more accurate. But he wanted her to accompany him from London to Arkansas and then on to New York City, and the Gulfstream had only one small bedroom. Post-coital separate sleeping arrangements were not possible. That had been her cue that it was now or never.

She was a mile down the trail. Better get this done now and then get back to the car. Tell the driver you don't feel well. Drop the journal under the bed as if it had fallen there. Get made up to look beautiful. Play your role. Mesmerize him. And hope Alexander never suspects you of treachery. He was always kind and patient with her, but she knew that was only a façade covering a dispassionate violence. She shuddered.

Pauline opened the portfolio. He had written in small carefully formed letters on almost every page. She remembered Burke's words and was just as glad she couldn't read the Greek alphabet.

I think it's Greek.

After five months with the man, she knew Burke was right. She didn't want to know what the words said. She wanted to be done with this business.

She pulled out her smartphone and took a picture of the first two-page spread. Burke had installed a special app that would upload each image to a secure website as it was shot. She fanned the pages and estimated she would take about fifty or sixty pictures. Ten minutes tops she hoped. Probably fifteen. Her stomach knotted and her hands began to shake as she moved to the second and third pages. Would the images be blurred? The camera was designed with a motion stabilizer, but she was really shaking. Not her problem if some of the pictures were fuzzy. She was the one with her neck on the line.

She shuddered. It was as if she could feel Jules' lifeless eyes on her now.

Just finish and make yourself look so beautiful that all Alexander can think about is being with you. On the plane. At dinner. The promise of the bedroom. Exploit his lust. Dump the portfolio under the bed when you get back to the plane. Let him think he dropped it there while getting ready this morning.

She heard a twig snap behind her and turned with a start.

A deer crossed the path and disappeared into the dense woods. She laughed uneasily. Her breathing was more ragged than when she was running.

She turned another page, centered the new spread on her screen and pushed the camera icon again. The sound of a shutter seemed to echo off the silence of the forest. Why do smartphone makers assume we need sound effects?

Another sound. She looked up. Nothing. Must just be the rustle of leaves in the wind. A trickle of sweat ran down her brow. She barely moved the portfolio in time to keep a salty bead from dropping onto the open page and smudging the ink on the nearly translucent surface. Alexander would have known someone was turning his pages. That would have been a disaster. That was too close.

She slowed her breathing, willing herself to calm down. Burke had taught her how to control her emotions by controlling her breathing. When had she ever panicked before? Her life had not been easy. Not as a little girl in a home with two ex-pat American alcoholics in Brussels and not since she had taken to the street to make a living turning tricks when she was fifteen. She had faced plenty of jams and always kept her poise. She had been in physical danger and instinctively found a way out. She had nearly killed a man by stabbing him in the stomach with a butter knife she snatched from a room service tray. Maybe she killed him. She never checked.

Maybe she would jam Alexander's precious Fulgor Nocturnus in his heart when this was all over. It would serve him right for making her feel so insignificant and expendable, despite his stern and chilly politeness.

All was silent again. She bent her head to the task at hand.

Aim, shoot, turn the page.

12

New York City

BURKE WANTED TO SCREAM IN exultation. Had she done it? Had she pulled it off? The green light on his iPad app signaled she was transmitting.

I think I love you Pauline.

Did he just think that? Did he love her? If so, he had a funny way of showing it. Realistically, when you combine a beautiful woman with tons of stress, you're sure to come up with crazy ideas.

Shut up, Burke. Keep your focus. You still haven't got her out of there. Get the goods. Get the girl. Then do a dance—and figure out how to keep her and yourself alive.

He had checked into a hotel in Harlem under one of his many names near the Columbia University Hospital. When he checked out of his hotel in Manhattan he had spent almost an hour walking, stopping, changing directions, descending steps into subway stations and bounding up the stairs a block away, watching for suspicious movements in the reflections of store windows, and other counter surveillance measures until he was absolutely certain he wasn't being followed.

Burke had inserted an app in Pauline's phone that instantly transmitted any pictures she took to a secure website with an invisible and encrypted IP address only he could access. From there it automatically forwarded to an equally secure web folder that could only be opened by whoever was paying him.

The man with the metallically altered voice who is trying to pinpoint my location.

His client wanted to be the first and only one to see anything found in Alexander' diary, but the fortune being paid wasn't enough to let Burke be careless, even with those paying the bills. He had done that once before. One false step and he was a dead man. Heck, he might be the walking dead already.

So he rigged the program to keep a copy of anything his client got for himself. Insurance.

Burke was raised in Nixa, Missouri, where he was taught each week in Sunday School to eschew the sin of greed—and run from a whole host of other temptations he had succumbed to as well. But greed might be what exactly was going to kill him before his time to face his Maker.

He stared at the screen, raising a cup of coffee to his lips. One image uploaded.

Keep going Pauline.

A second image. He put the coffee cup down and raised his fists in the air.

Don't stop now. I'll get you out of there if it's the last thing I do. Tonight.

The third image. He forced himself to stay seated, ready to bounce from wall to wall in the small room.

I won't even hire this job out completely. I'll be part of the extraction team myself.

Four. Five. Six.

Good work baby. We'll disappear after this is over. We'll have a long talk. We'll start from scratch.

If she was shooting two pages per shot, how many pages had Pauline sent him? Eleven? Maybe twelve?

He watched the screen breathlessly. Nothing. Maybe a slow satellite Internet connection? He started counting the seconds. Twenty. Twenty-one. Twenty-two. Twenty-three. Twenty-four. Twenty-five. Twenty-six. Twenty-seven. Twenty-eight. Twenty-nine. Thirty. Nothing.

Why had she stopped?

C'mon Pauline. Just aim and push the button. Doesn't have to be perfect.

He watched in stillness for another thirty seconds. Still nothing. Another minute passed. An excruciatingly long minute. His heart began to sink. He stood and stretched his back. He picked up a pillow and punched it. He slowed his breath and sat back down.

He scanned the images quickly. Two pages for every picture except for the first. He had just eleven pages in total. Surely the man wrote more than that in his leather journal. His client seemed certain that Alexander's journal was the Holy Grail of corporate espionage. Eleven pages? Had to be more.

What's happening Pauline? Why have you stopped? I know you aren't finished.

He stared at the short column of six static, unblinking icons on the computer screen. Even as he racked his brain for explanations he knew better. The program was failsafe. His stomach knotted up in a tight ball. He tasted bile in the back of his throat.

Pauline, I know you said yes of your own volition, but I'm sorry I put you in harms way. Just talk to me. What is happening Pauline?

13

Hodeidah, Yemen

NICKY MET HIS MAN AT a small café on the south side of Hodeidah, the closest town to the port of Mokha. He would like to be closer to the spot where he would climb aboard a speedboat to depart the dust and sand of Yemen, but the port only had one main pier with no commerce.

Platters of humus, grilled halloumi, tabbouleh, shish tawook, and dolma rested on the table between them. Nicky was ravished. He had lost fifteen pounds during his sixty-day tour of the Arabian Peninsula. He forced himself to slow down his chewing and count to five between bites. With a high speed boat ride ahead of him, he didn't want to sabotage his stomach's attempts to hold down the product of gestation.

The man across from him barely touched the food. His eyes smoldered in rage. He was the youngest son of Sheikh Sulaymon and the brother of the handsome Arabian prince who died at the hands of Malmak. Nicky was surprised the old man had sent Labeeb to acquire the precise location of Malmak and his warriors. Labeeb meant sensible and intelligent—two qualities that Nicky suspected the young man missed out on at birth. The kid was of an age to head to Europe or America for college, but he was a fanatic who didn't understand the long game. Why waste four or five years in study when you could be killing enemies of Allah and the tribe right now? The old man should know that there was a decent chance Labeeb would go Rambo and seek to avenge his brother in a solo kamikaze attack.

Nicky and his uncle fought over the same issues when Nicky was eighteen. In his case, he couldn't wear his uncle down. The fact that this kid was marching toward the front line of war rather than being secured on a safe university campus told him something about Sulaymon as well. He did not possess his uncle's strength and will. He doubted Sulaymon would be a player in the bloodbath that was to come. He was just one or two steps up the food chain from Malmak.

Of course, twenty years later, Nicky still forced his way to the front lines to his uncle's consternation. He looked at Labeeb closer.

He won't be alive in a week. Time for you to grow up and do your work from a distance.

What the kid did or didn't do was irrelevant to Nicky. One more casualty from a minor player in his uncle's grand drama was nothing.

What amazed Nicky most was that in exchange for telling Sulaymon where Malmak was encamped, he was bringing home a huge payday that would largely fund the weapons he had delivered to the man who had killed his eldest son.

That was the beauty of his uncle's plan. Pit both sides against each other. Let them do the dirty work—and pay the bill. Priceless.

Nicky would return the check for a bottle of beer or glass of wine to wash down the delicious local fare. Not smart and not possible. And it was definitely time to go. Every minute he remained on the peninsula was tempting fate. He had three men watching his back, including the Chechnyan military officer who deserted Malmak's camp the previous night.

"You aren't paying me enough to lose my head to a madman."

"Things are happening faster than planned," Nicky told him, giving him instructions on where to meet him in Hodeidah.

"Do I still get paid full amount?"

"Of course. And there will be more work for you soon. We'll leave together from the port. You'll go to Paris and await further instructions."

Nicky slid the sheath of papers across the table to Sulaymon's youngest prince. The kid studied the grainy night vision photographs carefully. He glanced at the summary page that gave the exact coordinates of Malmak's small military base.

"Tell me again how you got these—and why you are giving this information to us?"

Did Sulaymon give the young man instructions to ask these questions or was he thinking through all that had transpired in past two days on his own? He hoped the former.

"You already know how we came by this information. We are expanding our business in Yemen and are paying for information from many sources. You also know why we are passing on this information to your father. He is paying us a significant sum of money."

The young man's face was a mask of conflicting thoughts and emotions. It was obvious his suspicions weren't satisfied by Nicky's answers. But what could he do? How long would Malmak wait before moving against Sulaymon? He was there as emissary of his father. He had to make the deal. Nonetheless, Nicky gave an imperceptible nod to the Chechnyan. Be ready to shoot anything that moves, including the kid, if this goes south.

The young man scowled and slid an envelope across the table to Nicky.

"Do you want to verify the wire transfer details and instructions?"

Indeed, Nicky wanted him to, but knew everything would be in order. Sulaymon was not going to risk losing an immediate chance to avenge his anointed one. Nicky shook his head no, stood, gave a small bow, and answered, "Not necessary. I trust your father. I know that he knows what is at stake."

"As we trust you know what is at stake."

The two men locked eyes and glared at each other. Nicky almost wanted Labeeb to make a move at him so he could let the boy know his proper place in the universe. He knew what his uncle would do. Defer in order to win the battle that mattered. Nicky broke eye contact and nodded to the young man, granting Labeeb the victory.

Nicky hated to leave the uneaten food behind, but it was time to get out of Yemen with his head intact.

"It is a sin to waste food, Labeeb. Refresh yourself and then do your duty."

Labeeb was already out the door.

He and the Chechnyan walked to the door, checking all directions for ambushes. Nicky scanned upstairs windows across the street. Nothing. All was clear.

He took a quick step back in the café and grabbed a skewer of shish tawook before trotting out the door and jumping in the jeep to head for the pier.

14

The Isle of Patmos

IN GREEK AND ROMAN MYTHOLOGY, the Chimera combined parts of the lion, goat, and serpent to form a monster.

What better base to build a three-headed Chimera on than Ebola? First discovered in the Ebola region of the Congo, scientists knew that like rabies, salmonella, tuberculosis, Lyme, and a long list of other zoonotic diseases—diseases transmitted from animals to humans—it was hosted by an African animal. But which animal? Lyme came through tics, so treatments could be designed. But finding the exact source of Ebola wasn't nearly so easy to identify—and that made prevention and treatment protocols much more difficult.

More than thirty years after Ebola first grabbed international headlines no one actually knew its source and natural incubator. Despite spending hundreds of millions of dollars on research, scientists also didn't know how to treat the hemorrhaging disease that killed 80% of those it infected. Scientists still didn't know why some people survived it either. But that was a small matter, Dr. Claire Stevens thought. Close counted in horseshoes, hand grenades, and Ebola.

It met all reasonable standards of successful lethal application to major population concentrations.

The most significant research into Ebola, at least for her needs, was done in the Soviet Union in the 1980s and early 90s at the State Research Center for Virology and Biotechnology, secreted away in Siberia. While everyone else worked on a vaccine, Soviet scientists worked on finding a solution to weaponize Ebola. The exchange of bodily fluids within human contact was a wonderful conduit of disease but not efficient enough. It was too easy to stop through quarantine. To survive you simply didn't go near anyone bleeding their guts out and didn't let them near anyone else. Fifteen million people were going to die through mass quarantine with a new outbreak in West Africa—she didn't think, she knew—and that had nothing to do with their operation that was going to infect a new part of the world before anyone knew what was happening.

Before the collapse of the USSR, one of its best scientists had come close to putting it in an aerosol form. When the Berlin Wall fell signifying the death of the Empire, the program was disbanded.

Or so it seemed.

In 2004, Dr. Antonina Presnayakova, a scientist at the same facility, now privatized and heavily funded by American and European biotech companies, accidentally pricked her thumb with a needle laced with Ebola. She was purportedly working with Ebola infected guinea pigs to discover the elusive vaccine. She died ten days later, suffering convulsive hemorrhaging by herself in a quarantined white laboratory room.

Claire knew that Presnayakova was—despite the protests of conspiracy theorists—indeed working on a vaccine. But one of Presnayakova's colleagues, Dr. Dimitri Dolzhikov, had resumed working on the aerosol version—the weaponized version—and she knew for a fact that he had sold his documentation and his services to Claire's employer.

Her generous employer's identity was a secret to everyone in the Patmos labs, except for the director, Dr. Rodger Patton. Shortly after arriving, Claire proffered a guess, but the second she broached the subject with Patton, Rodger told her that such a line of inquiry was a certain path to termination. She wanted to ask what he meant by *termination* but held her tongue. That was the first time she understood the full implication of her decision to bring Mariama to the world. Did she regret it? Not in the least. Doing something great always conveyed a price. She kept her mouth shut on her suspicions.

It was irrelevant after she met Nicky. He was using a different first name and no last name. But she recognized him from a tabloid story she had read years before. Even before the pillow talk with Nicky began, she knew almost as much about their employer as Patton did.

Claire's specialty was biological chemistry and to the delight of the small team she worked with, she quickly made her mark by dramatically increasing the absorption rate of airborne Ebola. Her lab partners had already enhanced the Ebola strain with the addition of anthrax to increase the kill rate from eighty percent to almost ninety percent. They were killing chimpanzees like clockwork in the lab. But results in open air spaces were desultory, threatening the project's timetable.

She introduced an updated version of DMSO to the chimera. Dimethyl sulfoxide had little power to heal or harm in and of itself— though many a racehorse and Olympic athlete would swear to its effectiveness in reducing swelling and easing pain, thus speeding up the body's recovery process. But what was absolutely known was that nothing penetrated both membrane and tissue damage-free, aiding in the body's absorption of other medications, like the wood-based drug. It was so effective that any biological impurity in the ointment spread through the body like wildfire. It was a deadly disease's best friend. It was banned by the FDA in the United States for anything other than transporting human organs, though the European Union allowed broader uses. It didn't matter. Claire worked in a private lab located on a remote island in the Aegean Sea where it was impossible for curious eyes to figure out what they had and what they might be doing—how can you observe something you are unaware of?

That was another reason her team had an almost unlimited supply of chimpanzees and gibbons to work with. Those were the two primates most susceptible to the HIV/AIDs virus, the benchmark for contagion, which meant no other research animal was more important to an epidemiologist, no matter how politically incorrect it was to run tests on them—or kill them.

When she first mentioned adding DMSO to the recipe her colleagues looked at her like she was crazy and scoffed at the idea, even the legendary Dr. Dolzhikov, the man who had aerosolized Ebola to a nascent level. DMSO had to be in a topical form to be efficacious they protested. But to Claire it was a simple matter of cells and molecules.

When she killed a gibbon with the toxic spray in an outdoor setting, not even downwind, rare bottles of the 1988 Dom Perignon were uncorked with dinner and Dolzhikov was the first to toast her.

Her recruiter, Rodger Patton, was subdued that night. Was he jealous? Possibly. A typical male response.

The only downside of adding DMSO was that no matter how it was introduced to humans, there was an immediate—and mysterious—taste and odor of garlic. Even her synthetically enhanced variant reeked of the bulb. Maybe she would look for causes. Or not. The odor symptom would barely be noticed by those who were to experience its ability to deliver the biological payload.

Claire Stevens had always known she was smart but still marveled at things she knew and could do that few other scientists would ever experience. How sad and mundane for them. She was working on the vanguard of technologies that would change the world. Correct that. Save the world.

Stevens earned an undergraduate and master's degree in biology at University of Chicago. She stayed on Chicago's south side to get a

Ph.D. in biological chemistry. She then traveled south to Nashville to get a second Ph.D. in epidemiology from Vanderbilt University.

That was ten years ago. She left Vandy wanting to get her hands dirty saving the world. She landed an ideal job in Boston with an NGO, GlobalHope, which was associated with Harvard University and Massachusetts General Hospital. The NGO funded a state of the art medical research lab and annual get-your-hands-dirty fieldwork for the small team of scientists. The $65 thousand starting salary was paltry, but GlobalHope also paid off her student loans. Nine months in the lab, three months in the field, and constant access to the greatest research university and hospital in the world. What could be better?

Through hard work and an open mind, she discovered a cause and support system that was so much grander than raking in big bucks. Money never was her motivation.

Patience, Mariana. Our time is coming soon.

15

Devil's Den Hiking Trail, Ozark National Forest

THE SOUND OF RUSTLING AGAIN. Pauline looked up. Nothing. Her nerves had her imaging things.

Just finish and tell Burke to get you out. Tonight. Just be finished.

JULES HAD BEEN TRAINED TO stalk prey silently in all terrains and topography. Forest was the hardest. He left his shoes to the side of the trail a mile back. That helped his stealth. The problem was if she saw him coming and got a jump, it would be nearly impossible for him to run her down without shoes. He had watched her closely for the past six months. She ran like a deer. If she got a jump on him, he couldn't catch her—with or without shoes—and would have to call for backup. They would have to bring in freelancers, never as reliable, to mount a search. There would be uncertainty. Not good.

He would just have to assess what course of action was best when he reached her—or she reached him doubling back. Alexander would want to talk to her. That thought almost made him smile. That would be one interesting and painful conversation.

But nothing would be worse than her escaping into the woods with Mr. Alexander's property. Though he had warned Mr. Alexander that something wasn't right with his new girl, the man hadn't listened. If he had, Jules would not be treading silently through a lush forest in Northwest Arkansas in his bare feet.

That also meant Mr. Alexander was unprotected at the moment, something that made him equally nervous. Jules took pride in how well he did his job of protecting the man.

He needed to get a clean shot off.

CLAIRE'S STOMACH DID A SOMERSAULT and she thought she was going to vomit. Her hands were shaking.

I don't know if I can do this. I thought I could but maybe I can't.

This job was to be her exit from a life she had come to hate. There was a moment when she thought Burke would be the one to free her. That hadn't quite panned out. Him sending her to another man's bed was a pretty good clue that he wasn't the man she hoped he was. Now all she wanted was for him to reach for her so she could rebuff him. Or not. Why had the man she thought she might be able to trust drop her into the lion's den? Whatever she thought he might feel for her was all in her imagination.

Don't dwell on it. It will only add one more hurt to your pain-filled life. Just concentrate. If you want a new life, you must do this. There is no one else you can count on. No one. Same as always. You should be used to that. Live with it.

She took a long slow breath. She willed her nerves to calm.

I can do this.

She shifted positions, turned the page, lowered her head, and aimed. Before she took the picture, Pauline heard a *phhhht* of air and felt an explosion of pain in her shoulder. She fell forward and heard another deadly puff of air race by her head, followed by the sound of leaves and twigs crunching behind her. She looked up and saw Jules sprinting toward her, gun raised.

She rolled and scrabbled forward; desperate to do the only thing she knew might save her life.

Run.

16

New York City

BURKE KNEW THE DAY HE had become a new man—and not all for the better. June 25, 2003.

He spent a semester at the University of Missouri in Columbia. It was his first time away from the strict and protective world of his childhood in Nixa, Missouri, where there were two—and only two—approved activities: church and sports. Baseball in spring and summer, football in the fall, and wrestling in the winter. Church every Sunday morning and night, every Wednesday night if he didn't have a game, and all week if there was a revival.

The first and only time he drank beer before college, the girl from his church youth group got a pang of conscience and told her parents everything that happened. Her dad, a fellow elder in the church with Burke's dad, made a beeline to the small ranch house Burke grew up in. He didn't mind the hell his dad gave him that included a nice left jab to the jaw when he dug in to fight it out. It was his mom sobbing for days over the thought of him spending an eternity in hell.

He almost smiled at the memory. It was a different time in his life. Harsh ... but somehow sweet.

He wondered if his parents still thought of him. They would have to. Missing in action and presumed dead. There was a plaque for him in the lobby of Nixa High School and a headstone in the Nixa Memorial Gardens. He visited the cemetery once. But he didn't visit his parents. Would he ever see them again?

Unfortunately, his mother's worse fears had come to fruition. He had gone to hell and never come back. His was not a sweet life.

After getting booted from the University Missouri, Burke pursued the only option he could envision. He joined the Army. Even patriotic folks like the fine people of Nixa were never quite clear on whether joining the United States Army was an honor or punishment for a kid who had got himself into some trouble, drinking and fighting his way to expulsion from college.

It didn't take long for Burke to figure out that if you were going to do the military, you might as well do it right—if you're going to be a bear, might as well be a grizzly. He got on track for Army Ranger Training Brigade the day he left boot camp at Fort Leonard Wood in St. Robert, Missouri.

Sixty percent of Army Ranger prospects that begin in Fort Benning failed the 61-day combat course and were reassigned. The physical hardship, including sleep and food deprivation, was something you couldn't prepare for ahead of time. Heck, two-thirds of those who didn't pass muster never made it through the first month. Burke graduated with the William O. Darby Award, signifying he was the best of the best. The 3rd Battalion, 75th Regiment was deployed for the War on Iraq, but as they liked to joke, they took a wrong turn and spent two years in Afghanistan where they fought a series of harrowing battles against the Taliban.

His battalion was finally moved to the Iraq theater of operations two years later on April 25, 2003, but then George W. Bush ordered a cessation of major operations on May 1, just as they were landing.

Burke didn't need to have worry about job security.

On June 15, he was assigned to Operation Dessert Scorpion, still under the command of Colonel Arnold Grayson—"just call me

Arnie"—their job was to defeat remaining "non-compliant" forces in the "post-hostilities" phase of the invasion. One day they would deliver humanitarian aid to a village, the next day they would rain fire on forces still loyal to Saddam Hussein. Even a college dropout like Burke could understand the three simple principles of waging war against guerillas: identify, isolate, and destroy. Isolating enemy combatants was not always possible—using civilians as human shields was the enemy's best defense—but they were making lightning fast progress on destroying the Iraqi resistance.

The moment that changed his world came ten days into the operation. Burke got back early from a reconnaissance mission to the city of Najaf. The neighborhood where they were to find bad guys was already a rubble heap from internecine fighting the night before. No one complained about a day off from painstakingly slow movement from house to house and room to room, always wondering if you would be looking down the barrel of an automatic weapon.

His buddies wanted to stop for a very illegal beer at a very illegal bar—the black market was coming to life, a sure sign their efforts were not in vain, before returning to base. Burke hadn't had even a sip of beer since his college expulsion and wanted to head back anyway. He said he'd cover for the team and get back to HQ solo. Still a stronghold of former Republican Guards posing as bankers and bakers who transformed into cold-blooded killers at night, Burke made his usual wary and stealthy approach to a back entrance of their camp within a city. He still didn't know why he did it—it wasn't his job and others were doing a fine job of minding the perimeter—but he decided to take a circuit around the wire to make sure no hostiles were looking for a hole in their defenses. Maybe he was simply delaying his return to the boring routine of living in a confined space.

At one of the remote barricades he saw something he wasn't supposed to see. Colonel Arnie Grayson and two other commanding officers were loading two crates of M4s in the back of a truck. It

RISE OF THE BEAST

didn't look right—he'd never seen an officer loading crates—but he wouldn't have thought anything of it had he not got a good look at the man standing by the passenger door of the truck who stared straight ahead, puffing on a cigarette. Burke stepped back in the shadows and studied the face. He was sure of it. The man was a prime target to be identified, isolated, and destroyed by Operation Desert Scorpion.

Burke was smart enough to know that allegiances of individual Iraqis changed constantly and that he was a grunt who didn't know much of anything happening above his pay grade. So he kept what he saw to himself and made his way back to his platoon. He downed a Budweiser—his first in nine months—and trudged to the front gate with the others when they were expected.

But his antennae were up and Burke started watching what was happening inside the command center with the same intensity he watched what was happening outside the fence. When he overheard the extent of the shrinkage of M4s and other tactical gear from the battalion's armory, he knew he had to report the incident.

On a routine escort assignment to Baghdad, he filed his report to the MP ADCON unit. Little did he know that the colonel who received his statement was a fellow classmate of Colonel Grayson at West Point—and part of Grayson's scam to pocket a boatload of money in service to Uncle Sam. Two days later he and five other team members were dropped near the town of Tikrit. Their job was to destroy a way station for guerilla forces who rarely slept in one place more than a night or two.

17

The Isle of Patmos

D-DAY, CLAIRE THOUGHT. ARE YOU ready to do this? Are you comfortable forsaking the dreams you had when you joined GlobalHope? Think of all you did, think of what you were trying to accomplish when you worked the field for them. You were going to save the world.

The problem was the field. She got her hands dirty in the Zimbabwean cholera outbreak in 2008; then the West African meningitis outbreak in Burkina Faso in 2009; another cholera outbreak, this time in Haiti, in 2010; three trips to South Africa in 2011 through 2013 for a first-hand experience of the HIV/AIDS pandemic—the last great global biological catastrophe with a death toll of 30 million—and then to the Guinea Ebola outbreak in 2014. Trips to India were interspersed and too many to count.

It wasn't the horrors of disease that eroded her sense of compassion for the plight of the suffering over time. It was the hopelessness of the people themselves. What was an occasional smattering of death in the face of such everyday crushing ignorance, poverty, violence, and every other human dysfunction imaginable? When a society was already self-cannibalistic, what was a little disease or plague? Did it really make things much worse than they already were? It paved a faster way for some people to escape the pain of existence and enter the blessed sleep called death.

Claire Stevens had gone out to make the world a beautiful place only to discover how brutal and ugly it was. But worse yet, the status quo for most people was simply hopeless.

GlobalHope? What hope was there? There was simply no way to counteract the enormity of the malaise that trapped humans in organizational systems and patterns of thought that guaranteed every stinking day of their life span would be filled with misery. If nature wasn't attacking them, then they attacked themselves.

She had been to Calcutta and visited Mother Teresa's Missionaries of Charity. It was after the iconic saint's death, but her words and pictures adorned the walls and the sense of her purpose and presence was palpable. She wondered if the saintly woman ever stopped to evaluate the efficacy of her efforts. If not, didn't that make her a narcissist who acted on her own behalf? It was definitely not PC to speak against Mother Teresa, but really, how could she come to the conclusion that prolonging such a pathetic existence was an act of charity? What good had she and her sisters done? If the well-intentioned sisters weren't keeping score, Claire was. There were more orphans, sick, and poor than when the legendary nun started the international enterprise.

Claire was sure Mother Teresa was a great woman and meant well. But everyone meant well. Claire was results based. Show me how life is improved and I will crawl across broken glass to help.

What she was doing now would help. And nothing would stop her. The Patmos plans were not subject to the fickle whims of imperfect people. The key decisions had been taken out of the hands of the predators who despoiled existence. It was unfortunate that millions upon millions of victims would die as collateral damage, but for many that would be an improvement from their hellish existence.

Her parents were as proud to be atheists as was she. But she had attended church for exactly one week as a third grader. A neighborhood friend in Aurora, Illinois, birthplace of Ronald Reagan and not much else, invited her to Vacation Bible School at her church. It wasn't Baptist or Methodist or Catholic or any of the other more common church names and she wished she could remember what the church was called. It was a seminal event in her life. She was shocked— as were the neighbors who invited her—when her parents agreed to let her attend. As an adult, she laughed at how much they would have debated granting her their permission. But they finally determined it would show their openness and be a cultural experience for Claire. How right they were.

The theme of the week was Noah's Ark. Most of the activities and songs, crafts, and skits focused on cute cuddly animals. Claire remembered winning a gold fish for reciting a Bible memory verse: "Then God said to Noah, 'Yes, this rainbow is the sign of the covenant I am confirming with all the creatures on earth.'"

All these years later she still remembered it.

Noah sawed and hammered away. Frolicking animals marched to the big boat in pairs. The Flood didn't get mentioned until the last morning. It was almost an afterthought. Jolly Noah and his cute fuzzy animals were saved and got to see the first rainbow—with a giraffe as lookout, of course—as they landed their happy and adventure-filled boat on a lush green mountainside. Was she the only one that noted everyone else in the story was drowned? The image of crashing waves, bolts of lightning, and people frantically treading water, scrabbling for a handhold on the sides of the wooden boat, and gasping for air scared her as a little girl. What about the people? Though her parents never said it, she was sure what felt to her like trauma made them very happy. Especially since she never asked to attend church again.

It was in Guinea that the weight of human misery she had witnessed hit its critical mass and altered her outlook forever. But it wasn't just chronic pathogenic disease. It was the people themselves.

While treating a twelve-year-old girl, Mariama, for a nasty, weeping genital rash, Claire saw, not for the first time, all the evidence of sexual abuse. She looked up at the mother. The woman lowered her head and refused to meet her eyes. She looked over at the father, standing protectively in front of three more daughters. He had no problem making eye contact with Claire. The smoldering hatred in his eyes dared her to say something, do something. He was in a protective stance all right; he was protecting a psychotic pattern of behavior he saw as his right. And indeed, it was his right since no one lifted a hand to stop him.

It wasn't that event only, but it was in that singular moment that Claire's heart changed forever. She began thinking of Noah's Ark again. But not with horror but with … was it possible? Could it be? Hope? Maybe God—at least the concept of God found in an ancient legend— was right to wipe out the evil that man had become. She hadn't thought of those God drowned as evil. Words like stupid, foolish, incompetent, and chronically violent entered her mind. But looking at Mariama's father, proud, defiant, violent, she suspected evil might be the exactly right choice of words.

She had been conditioned in her upbringing and education to attribute colonialism and corporate exploitation as the causes for poverty, sickness, high infant mortality, nutritional deficiencies, unchecked violence, and other signs of a sick society. But her own eyes and heart told her that this was the way it had been, was, and ever would be for some people, whether touched by civilization or not.

Her mind turned from saving lives to eugenics. Not the kind of eugenics practiced by that crank Dr. Kevorkian, administering a lethal injection to one old cancer or Alzheimer's patient at a time. But mass eugenics. A good death applied generously. Claire began to dream of a new flood. In her dream she would ask God if she could help bring the waters.

She was still an atheist but felt her prayer had been answered when she met Dr. Rodger Patton at a conference in Boston later that year. As they swapped war stories about the various pandemic hot spots they visited, they sensed they might have met a kindred spirit in each other. So they verbally probed and danced and sparred around the topic of societies and people that would be better off dead than alive, both for their own sake and that of others on the planet. It was only when they wandered into a discussion of the 19th Century writings of Reverend Thomas Robert Malthus that the dam broke and let loose the roiling waters in their hearts to one another.

In addition to being a preacher, Malthus was an economist and demographer. He posited that the increase of population is necessarily limited by means of subsistence; that population does invariably increase when subsistence is increased; and that the superior power of population is repressed, and the actual population kept equal to the means of subsistence, by misery and vice. It was a quaint way of saying when too many people compete for resources all hell breaks loose.

What Claire and Rodger had set out to do in compassionate service to humankind, they concluded, was make everyone happy and fruitful by relieving them in some measure from their culturally-induced misery. Even if neither totally agreed with Dr. Thomas Malthus and later Malthusians on a set population number of nine, ten, or twelve billion inhabitants that the earth could sustain, both agreed the earth's population was already well extended beyond a number that would allow more than a small fraction of its inhabitants to flourish.

But Malthus didn't see the bigger picture. Even if Planet Earth could sustain another five, ten, fifteen, twenty billion people—what was the point? Did everyone deserve to live? Wasn't it obvious some cultures had been measured and found lacking? Shouldn't Mariama's father and his like be made extinct for the betterment of the world?

They continued the dance and laughed when they talked about the premise of a popular novel called *Dante's Inferno*. Why would someone so smart as the mad scientist villain in the book introduce a population-killing plague indiscriminately? That was so stupid. It was obvious, some cultures knew how to live. Others didn't. Simple math wasn't the answer. The Reverend Malthus was wrong on that. Kill half the population but keep the same percentage of dysfunctional people groups, and you were simply kicking the proverbial can down the road for your children or grandchildren.

A week later Rodger called her when she was driving home from work in her Toyota Prius. He was back in Boston. They needed to talk, he let her know. He invited her to dinner at Menton on Congress Street downtown. Over an eleven course meal, he told her that he had come into contact with an organization committed to doing something to make the world a better place for the living—more specifically those who were able to fashion a reasonably successful living. She asked the organization's name. He said there was no name. But she was being invited to become both a member and an employee of this cutting edge research organization.

A day later, she called in sick to GlobalHope, a first, and flew first class to Frankfurt, Germany. From there she bordered a private plane that was luxurious beyond anything she could have imagined. When she asked the pilot what their destination was he put a forefinger to his lips and made the shushing sound. They landed close to water and from there she was ferried in a luxurious speedboat to an undisclosed island. She was welcomed at the dock by Patton and another scientist with a thick Russian accent. She was given a tour of the most remarkable laboratory facilities she had ever laid eyes on. She was then interviewed for twelve straight hours by a woman who was the head of Human Resources for a company with no name. Patton simply advised her to be forthright. There would be no record of this meeting and no personal or professional repercussions if she wasn't hired or elected not to accept an offer of employment. Sometimes formal, sometimes casual; sometimes hostile, sometimes warm and encouraging; sometimes general and sometimes focused on specifics from her life; she was asked to account for every inch, every nook and cranny of her entire life story—and her feelings about the state of the planet.

She wasn't sure how she did when the interview abruptly ended. She suspected she had failed, something new for her, which made her nervous. But when she landed in Boston, Patton was already there, waiting for her with a limo driver. They were driven to a brick home that had been converted to law offices on Boylston Street. It was there she was officially offered a job with Aristotle Research Partners—the company did have a name, even if it was a front and no one actually used it. Her official assignment would be on the company's only active project: Patmos. When the attorney told her what her salary and living arrangements would be, she was shocked at how little she was being paid by GlobalHope. She immediately accepted and signed reams of paperwork dealing with trade secrets and confidentiality; non-compete issues, patent ownerships, and too many other legal terms to remember. Details of the actual project were vague but she knew where Patmos was going and what it was about. Her talks with Dr. Patton had been specific. At least five billion non-progressive people must be strategically targeted for death.

She moved from confusion to certainty that this was the right course for a viable future humanity. She would have signed for less than she made at GlobalHope. Money was never her motivation.

A week later she called her parents to let them know she would be off the grid for a while and would call when she could, but that she was more determined than ever to save the world.

Listening to them babble with childlike wonder and joy at what a wonderful daughter she was created a memory she cherished, but ridiculed at the same time. She had talked to them once a month for two years and missed them terribly. But it was a small price to pay for changing the course of world history.

The director of GlobalHope let her know how sad he and the rest of the small team of scientists would be to see her go after she marched in his office and turned in her resignation. But he knew with her intelligence, talent, and drive, she would make a huge difference in the world. She did her best to look sad and grateful.

He was right.

Yes I will make a huge difference in the world. I will dedicate my work to Mariama.

18

Devil's Den Hiking Trail, Ozark National Forest

JULES RETRACED HIS STEPS ANGRILY. His socks were in shreds and his feet were bruised and bleeding. He felt no physical pain, only the psychological pain of failing Jonathan Alexander.

He chased Pauline for at least five miles—unless she had broken from the path and he missed her. It was nearly impossible to track someone while running as fast as you can. He managed two more shots in her general direction after she bolted. Even as he pulled the trigger each time he knew the bullet would not find its mark due to the dense foliage protecting her as she wound in and out of turns on the wooded path.

She had stolen from the man and she had escaped him. How could that have happened? His approach shot hit her in the shoulder. Alexander wanted him to take her alive if possible. He heard her cry of pain. He saw the flash of fresh bright blood set against a bright green sports top as he pounded up the path toward her. He saw her fall to her side. He was sure she would be waiting for him, maybe in shock, to secure her capture when he got to the spot. Instead, all he found was her fanny pack, Mr. Alexander's journal, and her smartphone.

He immediately sprinted in pursuit. Not wearing shoes didn't help his speed, but Jules did not think he would have caught her anyway. Not unless she was hurt badly enough to collapse. No way of knowing.

When he had her dead to sights, she had shifted her body weight down on all fours and bent her head forward. Instead of placing a cartridge into the flesh of her hip and immobilizing her, he came much closer to a kill shot than he planned. If she had dropped any lower to do her treacherous work, he would have spun a bullet in one ear and out the other. That wouldn't have been good. Mr. Alexander wanted her alive for questioning.

What to do now was the only question. The small team that accompanied Mr. Alexander wasn't prepared to launch a hunt through the woods. In Alexander's estate outside Geneva, the security team kept a small fleet of modified Trimble Gatewing X100 drones in the air as part of their security protocol. He was not sure whether Erich had packed one of the unmanned aerial machines in the hold of the Gulfstream. He should know. But how was he to anticipate needing it for a manhunt? The model was illegal for private use in the US, which probably meant it hadn't been stowed. Even if Erich did bring it, it would take an hour for him and his copilot, Michael, to arrive at ground zero. That was assuming they could immediately find an available car. The drone had a maximum of forty-five minutes of flight time. At eighty kilometers per hour, it could travel about fifty-three kilometers in the search for Pauline.

But what if Mr. Alexander's small team hadn't traveled with the drone? By calling Erich he would be broadcasting the full extent of his failure, the one thing Mr. Alexander didn't handle well.

Jules thought of covering up what had happened. He could just tell Mr. Alexander he had no choice but to kill her. But that would only prolong the inevitable revelation that she had escaped. She wasn't dead after all. Ultimately he knew only one thing: obedience. Jules sighed, pulled his satellite phone from a hip holster, and called Erich.

"Yes Jules?"

"Do we have the Gatewing with us?"

"We do not. Is there a problem?"

"Yes there is."

He explained the situation to Erich, ended the call, and hit the speed dial for Mr. Alexander. The conversation was short but painful.

"Bring in help and find her," were Alexander's final instructions.

He would put on shoes, get some equipment from his pack he had hidden near the trailhead, and would start back up the winding path with a high beam flashlight to look for signs of Pauline's movements.

Implacable, stoic, and confident, the only time Jules felt the sense of failure he did now was when he got the letter from the Roman Catholic Diocese of Basel, informing him he had not been selected for the Swiss Guard in charge of protecting the Holy Father and the Vatican. He was certain he would be selected. He met all the qualifications: he was Catholic, handsome, physically fit, a Swiss citizen, had military training and combat skills, and was between the ages of nineteen and thirty-one.

Some claimed the Swiss Guard was the finest fighting force in the world. What an honor that would be. He passed the physical tests with flying colors. But then the rejection letter arrived. When he pressed for an answer on why he was passed over, a nervous bishop who found Jules waiting for him in his office unannounced, let it slip out that Jules had not passed the psychological testing.

The Holy See's loss was Alexander's gain.

So how could he have let down the man who gave his life purpose and meaning?

I will find her. When Mr. Alexander has what he needs, I will cut out her eyes for my collection.

19

Bentonville, Arkansas

ALEXANDER'S MIND TRAVELLED BACK TO the first man he killed in cold blood. Everyone called Alexander, Jonto, at the time. He was only fifteen years old, working on a shipping vessel that was delivering cargo from Athens to Marseilles. There was a large wooden crate not listed on the manifest. Amongst the omnipresent barrels of olive oil, it concealed a few identically marked drums filled with snowy white powder wrapped in clear kilo packages. He and the man who hired him, Gabriel Lefebvre, were instructed to fit in with the other hands. There was a predetermined time and place where they would transfer the product to two men who would load the heroin on a freighter bound for Liverpool.

Under cover of darkness and fog—a smuggler's most beautiful kind of night—he and Lefebvre moved the heavy drums in a rowboat. The handoff went beautifully. But when they returned to their ship the second mate was waiting at the top of the ladder for them. He was also the ship's medical doctor and watch keeping officer. Either he was personally vigilant at all hours of the night or he had been tipped off by a crewmember that Alexander and Lefebvre were up to something.

The second mate confronted the two men alone. Big mistake. He informed them that all he wanted in return for graciously ignoring what

Lefebvre and Jonto had just done was their full cut of the transaction. Every penny. He let them know they should feel lucky he hadn't already manacled them together in the brig to turn over to the police at the next port. A bigger mistake. Despite his youth, Jonto was not someone to threaten unless you were willing and ready to act immediately. It would have been much wiser for the ship's watch keeping officer to threaten him after he was restrained.

Gabriel stood slack jawed and submissive. Quick as a snake, Alexander gutted the man with a switchblade, spilling his blue, gray, and purplish intestines and a bucket of bright red blood slippery goo on the deck. He wiped both sides of the knife on his pants, snapped the silvery razor-honed blade in its holder, and pocketed it.

"What did you just do?" Gabriel whispered, dark eyes gleaming, barely able to control the quaver in his voice.

"The only thing there was to do," Jonto answered calmly. "The man was going to steal what is ours."

"*Vous tromper!*" Gabriel hissed, pushing Jonto backwards.

Already playing the long game, Alexander was patient and slow to anger even at this young age, but he would not suffer anyone to call him a fool without consequence.

The second man he murdered was Gabriel Lefebvre. Two seconds after he hissed *"vous tromper!"* at him, Alexander slashed Gabriel's throat, the knife retrieved from his pocket and opened with near magical speed. Lefebvre stared at Jonto in astonishment through lifeless eyes before slumping atop the second mate on the bloody deck. Alexander took Lefebvre's cut of the fee from the inside pocket of his oilskin windbreaker and relieved the second mate's corpse of the generous wad of francs and other currencies in his wallet. He threw both men overboard and went back to the crew's sleeping quarters for his rucksack. He quietly climbed down the ladder, checked that all his belongings were collected, slung the heavy pack over his shoulder, returned above deck, descended the ladder to the rowboat, untied it, and launched away from the ship, putting all his strength into a slow but steady stroke. When he stepped ashore, Jonto began the long journey back to Greece by road.

The big boss, the man who hired Alexander after his father died wasn't happy with him for killing Lefebvre and damaging a longstanding business arrangement. But Petrov Xenakas saw something in Alexander's eyes that he knew could be used. By seventeen, Alexander—still named Jonathas Alexopolous and known as Jonto to his friends—was a bodyguard and enforcer for a Greek heroin smuggler.

Alexander almost smiled when he thought of the final moment when he seized Xenakas' empire from him, killing him with the same switchblade he had used on Lefebvre and the second mate that fateful night on the Mediterranean.

Were there any murders he regretted? Holding the pillow over the jaundiced face of his brother, Nikolai, while he was in a drunken stupor had been a little painful. But Nikolai's drinking and gambling habits had become too hard to manage and were costing the Alexopolous syndicate too much money. The booze had killed him already anyway. No, he didn't regret that murder, and wasn't sure it should be considered murder anyway.

But now, what of Reverend Garrison? Was it bad luck to order the execution of a good luck charm?

The man had served his purpose. All he could do now was complicate an already complicated undertaking.

No, Garrison had to die. But perhaps when the second phase of Patmos was underway, he would build a memorial for his spiritual mentor.

"IS EVERYTHING OKAY, SIR?" THE driver asked.

"What could be wrong on such a lovely fall day?" Alexander responded pleasantly. Inside he was irritated that his state of mind was so easy to read—and that he was being studied with perhaps a flicker of recognition. He was preoccupied and hadn't replaced his sunglasses and hat. He needed Jules at his side.

"You are right on that. It is a beautiful fall. I apologize for asking, sir."

"No apologies, please, that was kind of you to ask," Alexander answered smoothly. "And it was kind of you to be so accommodating to drive Jules out to meet our friend at the trailhead."

"Just my job, sir. Very happy to do so. Is one of our drivers coming back for them or is another service picking them up? I heard Samuel, her driver, was given the last part of the day off. Heck, I could drive back down there myself if no one is scheduled yet."

"Again. That is kind of you ..." Alexander located the man's name on his printed itinerary ... "Charles. But your offer won't be necessary. We've made other arrangements."

Alexander pulled his sunglasses from his lapel pocket and pushed them over his nose. He kept his face pointed straight forward but watched the driver's eyes dart nervously between the road and the rearview mirror. The chauffeur's eyebrows moved back and forth, up and down, in a rhythm of deep thought. He is trying very hard to figure something out, Alexander thought. I don't like to be presumptuous, but I suspect he wonders why I look familiar and who I am.

"So you'll be going to the airport alone, sir?" the driver queried.

Today is not the day to have a driver who is curious and inquisitive, Alexander thought. Particularly with Pauline wounded and at large. Jules would do all he could to reacquire her but there was a vast expanse of territory to cover. The trail Klaus found for her was in a state park consisting of thousands of acres. The problem was exacerbated in that it abutted the Ozark National Forest. Pauline had become the proverbial needle in a haystack. Support, including men and drones, was en route, but a lot could happen before their arrival throughout the evening.

He looked forward. Charles was circumspectly watching him in the rearview mirror. He needed to assuage the driver's meddlesome concern.

"My traveling companion has been training for her first triathlon. As soon as she started up the trail, she became quite taken by the scenery and topography of your area. I suggested she stay over a couple days to take advantage of this lovely setting."

"I've never understood those distance runners," the driver commented. "My daughter ran cross country in high school. It looked like nothing but pain and sweat to me."

"I could not agree with you more, Charles. Triathletes, marathoners, and the like are different animals. Once she decided to stay for some altitude and hill training, she insisted it begin with today's run. Young people are so bold and fearless. I had to insist with her that Jules remain to make sure she's safe and to organize suitable accommodations for her stay. I would love to stay over myself, but business calls."

I'm afraid I need to give another task to Jules, Alexander thought. Jules knows how to simulate a fatal heart attack and another dozen ways to make a death look like natural causes. But he must move fast and still be particularly circumspect as we are on foreign soil and have other acute problems to wrap up.

Alexander's mind began to take inventory of the day.

Reverend Garrison, I thank you for your spiritual counsel. You were most helpful today even if I am still not sure if God, if he indeed exists, will work on my behalf. If he doesn't or if he works against me, I know the one who will cover my efforts with spiritual protection. I am sorry the blessing you provided for me will cost you so much. But great deeds require great sacrifices.

Pauline, you were a bad girl. But be assured, Jules will find you. Not even I want to know all that he will do to you.

Alexander almost smiled. Then he furrowed his brow. No one was supposed to know he was in Northwest Arkansas. His publicist made sure a few members of the paparazzi knew he had landed in Nice, France, with a young runway model from Milan. His publicist actually believed that was true. As did the runway model. Alexander didn't hold the prejudice that pretty girls weren't smart, but in this case, she was clueless that the man who was wining, dining, and bedding her, was Alexander's doppelgänger. But others, undoubtedly enemies, now knew better.

Loose ends are annoying … but inevitable. So no matter. Every day has its problems. Nothing we can't handle. We knew this was going to be arduous, so nothing has changed.

CHARLES, THE CHAUFFEUR, KEPT HIS eyes on the road. He made a conscience effort to stop glancing at the man behind him. He chewed on his lower lip, a nervous habit his wife hated, as he tried to sort out the day's events.

His passenger's words on his companion—*I think we know what kind of companion she is*—wanting to stay over for further training were strange. The deadly, blond gorilla told him she was going to take it easy because she wasn't feeling well. She wanted to go straight back to the jet and wait for another car after she walked back to the trailhead.

I told him it was best for me to wait at the trailhead and send another car for the old man, but the bodyguard insisted I come back to the church. That didn't make sense either.

Despite his concerted efforts to keep his eyes straight ahead, Charles looked at his passenger in the rearview mirror yet again. He couldn't see the man's eyes through the darkened lenses, but he felt an intense eye contact with the man, whoever he was.

I should know his name. I've seen him before.

Charles felt a prickly tickle run from his scalp to the back of his neck. He released an involuntary shudder of fear that raced from the top of his head to the tips of his toes.

Why is he staring at me? What is he thinking? Who is this creepy guy? It feels like he is in my mind.

20

Arlington, Virginia

"ANY CHANCE WE GOT EVERYTHING?" Grayson asked.

"If Alexander wrote only eleven pages in his journal then we for sure got it all," answered the young man furiously tapping on a keyboard in front of a wall of monitors.

"I'm not in the mood for your sarcasm," Grayson snarled. He didn't like the informal communication style of young people today, which was anyone under forty in his book. He particularly didn't like this young man's constant stream of flippant remarks. He missed his days in the United States Army when he could plant a boot where the sun didn't shine to cure a young man of his character and attitudinal deficiencies.

"Sorry, sir. What I meant to say is what we already know. The transmission stopped on a page that was in midsentence. Right after it started. Our man didn't get all of it."

"So no chance the satellite connection was broken and we'll get the rest later?" Grayson asked as he ran a hand over the gray stubble of his military haircut. Ramrod straight, he was a compact five-eight and one-hundred-and-sixty pounds of muscle and sinew that belied his sixty-two years of age.

"No sir. Not a couple hours after it started. At least I don't think so," Mark Doyle, the mid-thirties, nearly emaciated programmer answered, wanting to roll his eyes and say something smart, but wisely resisting.

"Diagnostics showed everything arrived at burst speed fine," Doyle continued. "Nothing else was sent. Nothing is lost in the Deep Web," he added.

He knew Colonel Grayson—the man loved the title so much he had made Colonel his first name—was very proud that he knew about the part of the Internet that was not indexed by common search engines and where Doyle and other hackers and spies did much of their work. Doyle gave Grayson just enough information to make him feel like he understood something he was totally ignorant about.

After a pause, Doyle mustered his courage to continue, "There's one other thing I've discovered, sir."

What now Grayson wondered.

"I don't like the way you're saying 'one other thing,'" he said softly, but in what he knew from experience was a menacing tone.

Doyle had grown inured to the old man's temper and tirades but did his best to look scared. The colonel liked intimidating people. Doyle would love to give the old man "one more thing" but the old fart paid him too much to stir that hornet's nest. Maybe he would screw with the colonel's credit cards when this contract was up.

"Well?" Grayson asked calmly.

"We're not the only ones that got the transmission, sir."

"What?!" Grayson bellowed, the calm instantly replaced by rage.

Here we go again, thought Doyle. Rant and rave like your hair is on fire. I can wait. I hope you pop a blood vessel and send a clot to your brain.

After a pause, Doyle said politely, "It's got to be your operative, sir. He was the only one that could have created a back door in our program. It was in his possession for more than nine months."

Burke. What game was he playing? Grayson asked himself, his eyes burning holes into the soul of his computer hack.

Grayson was one of the few men in the world that knew the real identity of the shadowy international fixer. He had followed the career of the man who had once served under his command with interest and admiration. At times he almost thought of Burke as the son he never had. Grayson actually had a son, an attorney, but he didn't really care for him. Too soft. Grayson sent business Burke's way on a regular basis. He didn't think Burke had a clue that the steady stream of work that flowed his way was anything but organic.

But this was the first time he had employed him directly. What a disappointment. He knew the task was herculean, near impossible, but based the Burke's previous—and sometimes improbable—successes, Grayson thought Burke had the tenacity and savvy to pull it off. What a miscalculation. The time it had taken Burke to reach the point where he screwed up the acquisition of Alexander's secrets was ridiculous. It wouldn't be a reflection on Burke with Grayson's employer. His employer didn't know about Burke. It would shine a spotlight squarely on him. Unacceptable. Burke's failure was ultimately his own failure. The buck always stopped at the top.

What had gone wrong? Why was such a simple task so hard? Grayson didn't know every detail of the operation, but had kept his eyes and ears on the basics from a distance, and knew Burke had laid a classic honey trap for Alexander.

Why do smart men fall so easily for pretty girls?

Little did Burke know that Grayson had helped him with that detail.

Alexander's life was so structured and guarded that getting into the journal was impossibly slow work, which magnified the failure to secure anything more than a prologue—a strange, rambling, insane prologue—of what Alexander was planning next in his illustrious international career.

"I will ride the blood red horse of the Apocalypse? I will be the Beast?"

What the hell was Alexander planning to do? Grayson wondered. Get saved? Start a religion? If so, the man had a peculiar understanding of faith. The tortured prose made it sound like he had plans to wipe out more than half the earth's population. Was he experiencing dementia? There was a rumor Alexander suffered a stroke in the past few years. The scribbling in his diary had nothing to do with business plans as Grayson's client had led him to believe would be the case. The mumbo jumbo in the opening pages of that leather journal was crazy talk. He started with a computerized translation of the script and then had a Georgetown linguistics professor who was fluent in Classical, Koine, and Modern Greek, rush over to make sure he got the translation right. Grayson read the corrected words at least ten times. They made little practical sense, unless the man really was planning mass genocide, which you never knew with an ego the size of Alexander's. Was he? If so, he was a fool. That couldn't be right. The man was not stupid. He knew math.

If countries with nearly unlimited budgets couldn't figure a way to eliminate a couple billion undesirables, how could one man? Sure he was the rich of the rich. But even if he threw ten or twenty or whatever billion dollars he had sitting around at the task, that would only go so far as was evidenced in Washington, D.C., which couldn't get a bang for a trillion bucks, home of his longtime employer at the Pentagon, and the source of most of his work as an independent contractor in the world of international espionage.

Doyle watched Grayson's face contort in agitation. It was almost amusing. He waited silently for his next orders.

Grayson looked over and their eyes met. What about the kid? Doyle, the MIT grad, was plenty smart. When it came to computer programming he was a genius. He definitely needed a sandwich and some exercise if he was going to get rid of the death camp survivor look.

Poor guy. Wonder if he's ever had a date, much less got laid. I should have at least got him a hooker to help realign his maladjusted outlook on life. Might have knocked some of that sarcasm out of him.

A genius, but apparently Doyle was not bright enough to protect the operation from the only thing that mattered. Other eyes. Traces of what they had done. Grayson was working for a whale who was himself dangerous. But not as dangerous as the man he wanted Grayson to extract information from. A much larger whale with the teeth of great white shark. There was a reason he had subbed out the project to Burke. Grayson wanted to stay nimble if something went wrong. And it looked like something had gone seriously wrong.

Why am I surprised?

He looked over at the kid. What was his first name? Matt? He knew too much and had proven to be unreliable, not just in work but also in attitude.

"I'm sorry, sir," Doyle said earnestly, doing his best to hide the joy he felt at his employer's discomposure.

"You did your best Matt," Grayson said laying a comforting hand on Doyle's shoulder.

"It's Mark, sir."

"So sorry, Mark," said Colonel Grayson.

In a fast, vicious, practiced twist of his hands, Grayson snapped the man's neck, severing his spinal column cleanly.

What's one more mess to clean up in an operation that had been a disaster from the start?

But this was less of a mess than letting the kid live. Who was he kidding? Failure meant a contract on his head. Time to shut this thing down before he found himself standing still while someone put him in their crosshairs. Time to let it go and move on.

Grayson hated to admit what had been on his mind. Maybe there were waters too deep to swim in even for a man of his prodigious skills and accomplishments. Maybe he was being too hard on Burke. When the full contents of Alexander's journal failed to deliver, it was a sure signal that it was time to exit the stage, something he had been planning anyway. Burke wasn't the only one who had created a life in the shadows with enough identities, tripwires, protective layers, and cold hard cash to live out retirement in luxurious comfort. Grayson would miss the adrenaline rush of the battlefield, but all good things must come to an end. Maybe he'd get to know his grandkids. But probably not.

He hated to retire on a failed operation. But survival was the ultimate victory.

Doyle's empty eyes looked up at him.

What'd you say Mark? Speak up! Nothing to say? No sarcasm?

Before he disappeared—his first retirement destination would be Argentina with all those pretty young girls, he thought—he needed to take care of a few loose ends; one in particular. Who was the man that had hired Grayson going to look for when it became obvious he wasn't going to get what he paid for? Himself of course. Twenty-five million US dollars should get you a lot more than eleven pages of drivel.

I will be the Beast? What are you thinking Alexander? I knew this would be a SNAFU—but this is over the top messed up.

Grayson didn't want to look over his shoulder for the rest of his life, wondering when the man who hired him—or the man he tried to steal from—would finally locate him. He, Grayson, had to die. Correction. He needed to appear to die. And he had to put the man who hired him on the trail of the man who killed him. That would be Burke. But he didn't want the man to actually find Burke. So Burke had to die in reality, but appear to have survived. Burke had eluded a death Grayson planned for him once before. But this time he wouldn't be so lucky.

Burke was a shadow in the world of shadows, but hadn't yet figured out his every move had been monitored the past six months, thought Grayson, a twinkle in his eyes. Burke didn't know that Grayson knew he had switched hotels in a hurry. He didn't know that Grayson knew he was in the Oak Room at the Plaza Hotel pretending to drink a vodka tonic right now.

I'm sorry son. To think, after this was all done I was going to hand you the keys to my business. But failure is not an option. For either of us. Someone's got to pay. It sure as hell ain't going to be me.

21

The Mediterranean Sea

DAD ALWAYS WANTED ME TO wear a suit and work in an office, Nicky Alexander pondered. Maybe he was right—or maybe I'm getting older. Or maybe I've got someone on my mind … no … don't go there … better to keep your mind off her. Keep your thoughts on what matters.

After the conclusion of his frontline work in the baking sun of Yemen and Saudi Arabia, he slipped into Sudan on a speedboat across the Red Sea. Not quite as dramatic as Moses, but it felt like salvation after his time with Sheikh Malmak. His earlier meetings there held the same purpose as his time with the old buzzard, but none held the same drama or danger. Still, his uncle was right. He had built a formidable network of stooges who didn't have a clue why they were being given armaments and vital information about their enemies, but knew exactly what to do with the mother lode of resources. It was time for him to let others do the nasty work.

After taking a jeep across barely passable desert roads, he caught a plane from Khartoum to Cairo under one of his aliases. Rubbing the stubble on his head and catching the reflection of his black beard in a window before boarding, he wasn't sure his own mother would recognize him, much less the sailors on the merchant marine vessel he was working on out of Port Said to Port Chania on the Island of Crete. He was just another itinerant worker looking to make a few bucks loading and unloading freighters.

From Crete, he would take a commercial ferry filled with budget tourists that made a stop in Patmos, his next stop. From there he would find out how his operations were progressing and get his next assignment from Uncle. Flying under the radar, he felt naked not knowing what was happening in Yemen, the Ukraine, the States, Liberia, Shenzhen, Turin, Paris, Berlin, London, Moscow, and other areas strategically targeted for beta events.

How long will I get to stay in Patmos? Better not to think of that. His uncle would not approve. But thoughts of the remarkable scientist, Claire Stevens, beautiful and fair in contrast to his dark, hard handsomeness—or so he had been told—were impossible to suppress.

He knew the first time he laid eyes on her that he wanted her—and that she wanted him. The chemistry was intense and magical. How many women had he slept with? Too many to count. But nothing compared to unbridled passion of making love to Claire. No, not quite right. Making love *with* Claire.

Is that a first for me?

He focused on what mattered most. He would make calls on a satellite phone that bounced to various stations in space to catch up on developments. Only then would he allow one of the medical staff to attend to the jagged wound on his forearm. People would whisper that he had to fight his way out of Yemen, but the truth was he was gashed opening crates of Kalashnikovs—a mere scratch in comparison to the American and the Saudi prince's neck injuries. Then he would take a long hot shower to clean the ubiquitous desert sand that had burrowed itself in every nook and cranny of his body. Next he would visit the Patmos barber—his uncle had brought in the man who had cut his hair as a kid—for a straight edged razor shave. Then he would take the forbidden walk down the hall to Claire's apartment. They would share a shot of ouzo followed by a simple dinner and bottle of Agiorgitiko wine. Then the evening would begin.

Now is not the time to think of such things.

One thing Uncle had always taught him was business first. Always.

Malmak, if you are only half the man you think you are, you truly are great and mighty. Attack before they arrive at your camp. Bring the dawn of war to the southern reaches of the Saudi Peninsula. Then die. I hope you choke on your qat as the blood drains from your body.

"Hey, we aren't paying you to look at he sea," the angry Moroccan shouted at him. "I'm docking your pay."

He shoved Nicky backward. Nicky nearly bit his tongue, squelching the impulse to strike back. He lowered his eyes and mumbled an apology. He quickly bent to hoist and carry a heavy crate into the ribbed metal container that was being prepared for delivery at Port Chania. The man smacked him in the back of the head.

Nicky took a deep cleansing breath and stifled a smile. In the world he worked in, it was wonderful to be taken lightly. That meant you were invisible—and alive to greet another day.

Suddenly the roar of a sleek black helicopter descended from above. The foreman ordered men to make space for the rotating blades as it pitched and bobbed onto the white painted crosshairs of the helipad.

The captain was now on deck and strode forward to greet the man who quickly exited the craft. Nicky knew him immediately. Frank Wallach was a captain in his uncle's military division. There could be only one reason for his appearance. Nicky stepped forward.

"Get back, scum," the Moroccan threatened with raise hand.

"Let him through," the captain snarled, giving the man a boot in the buttocks as he turned to back away.

The supervisor stepped back with bowed head to let Nicky pass.

He and Frank embraced.

"What's happening? Where are we going?" Nicky asked Wallach as they jumped aboard the helicopter.

"A small setback," Wallach said, as they lifted off the deck of the freighter. "You're meeting Mr. Alexander in New York City. Tonight."

The blues and greens of the Mediterranean were stunning as the freighter became a speck in the undulating, white-crested lines and swirls on the canvas of water.

So much for being invisible, Nicky thought. And so much for seeing Claire. He nearly groaned with yearning.

22

Tikrit, Iraq
June 25, 2003

THE MEN DROPPED ON CABLES from the UH-60 Black Hawk helicopter at dusk. The shooting started before they hit the ground.

Even as he dropped and rolled behind a stony outcrop, Burke's mind whirled. If they knew we were coming, they would have shot down the Black Hawk. That weapon of death was a much bigger prize for Saddam's resistance forces than the bodies of five Rangers.

Burke poked his head above the rocks to assess how bad the quagmire he had landed in was. The rocks in front of him exploded with gunfire. Bad.

He was twenty years old and certain he was dead. He saw all four of his assault team members dead or dying where they landed. A platoon of fifteen enemy combatants was fanned out in an approach formation, less than a hundred yards from where he was crouched. One football field separated him and death.

Burke thought of his parents and the little church he grew up in. This was the moment you prayed. You asked God to forgive you and make sure you were ready to meet your Maker. Even an atheist covered his bases. But his mind continued to race.

If they knew we were coming, they would have blasted us out of the air with Russian-made SA-21 Growlers. But they knew we were coming—and they didn't. Something was seriously amiss.

Burke couldn't say the prayer. If everything he had been taught was correct, he was accepting eternity in hell. But he was already there. He was filled with a raging hatred that wasn't a good starting point for talking to God.

Burke rolled to his left and fired his M4 at the left flank. Two men dropped, bright red wounds on their chests. He immediately rolled to the right and dropped three men on the left flank. Five men down. Ten to go. Not good odds now that they knew he was alive and returning fire. He wanted another look to see what was happening, but already knew they were moving fast to outflank him.

Their approach had been careless. They weren't expecting opposition.

He looked behind him at a small drop and made a simple tactical decision. Run into the desert.

But he knew he had to do something first. Ranger honor said you left no man behind. The men who fought together outside the fence knew that was not precisely correct. You didn't leave a live man behind to be tortured. He knew his mates would do the same kindness for him. He popped his head out and finished off the only teammate who was still moving. He had many regrets in life, but this act of mercy wasn't one of them.

Then Burke sprinted a zigzagging pattern the first hundred yards from the rock cropping while bullets sprayed behind and beside him. When the sounds of Kalashnikovs died down, he settled into a steady six-minute mile pace.

Why aren't they chasing you? He knew the answer. They assumed he was good as dead—and that's what they had been prepped and paid to do. Keep running and live to face another day.

Where would he end up? He had no idea. He knew getting as far away from the platoon HQ and Colonel Grayson was priority number one.

Sometimes you can't go home.

New York City
The Present

"GET FIVE MEN TO TEETERBORO. If she's on his plane, we jack the car and pull her out now. If she's not on the plane, I want to know where the car goes. The operation ends tonight."

He hung up the second the man grunted confirmation. His next call was to Henri.

"Yes, boss?" the Frenchman answered sleepily.

"Time to move offices, Henri. Keep the line open to Pauline and to me, but clean everything else up and switch locations. Tonight, if possible."

"What's happened boss? Is Pauline okay?"

Burke didn't respond.

"Sorry boss. I know better. No questions. I'll shut things down in Luxemburg. I'll head to Brussels and await word."

"Don't tell me where you're going," Burke responded curtly, disconnecting the call.

Henri looked at the phone dourly. He hated what he was about to do. He liked Burke. They had gotten in and out of some tough jams together. Burke was a good guy. He was loyal in a world of treachery. But someone offered to pay him more to keep him abreast of Burke's plans and movements. A lot more. Henri hit the preassigned number for a call to Arlington, Virginia.

BURKE WAS ANGRY. WHY was Henri being so sloppy? Burke himself was already breaking every security protocol and didn't need more breaches in his leaking ship. He could feel the water rising.

Burke looked at himself in the mirror. Jeans. White shirt. Simple black cashmere jacket. There was a Sig Sauer holstered at the small of his back. He wasn't prepared, but what he had on and what he packed was good enough for where he was heading.

It would have to be or more people close to him were going to die.

23

The Ozark National Forest

THE TEMPERATURE WAS DROPPING. PAULINE'S shoulder alternated between numbness and throbbing agony. She didn't know how far she had run. Maybe ten miles. She had no clue what direction she was heading or how close to help she was. She had no phone, no identification, no food, no medical supplies, no outer clothing, and no cash. Her running gear was top of the line, but it wasn't made to keep her warm overnight while exposed to the elements.

If I go to sleep out here, there's a good chance I won't wake up. They will have won.

She was walking now. Stumbling was a better description.

What was she going to do? She had no way to contact Burke. She never saw the numbers for him or the bakery she called. It was all programmed in her phone. She had a good memory but there was nothing to remember. A blank screen was all that appeared on her phone when she called. She had no contact information for her handler. Burke said it was safer that way.

I'm sure you are right. But safer for who, Burke?

She knew Jules would be leading a search for her. She still couldn't believe she had escaped him. The trail was an upward winding climb, surrounded by dense forest. Pauline had never considered herself to be an environmentalist, but maybe she would become one. It was the trees and ground foliage that had saved her life after all.

I escaped certain death but how do I stay alive to celebrate it?

Even if she found an egress from the forest and wandered onto a road at the very moment a police car was driving by, that would still be a death sentence. She didn't know the details of how they did it, but she knew the big picture of how Alexander and his minions worked. They were connected. They knew things—whatever things they wanted to know. Their ears were to the ground right now. They would know when she surfaced on the grid of civilization.

Why did the universe let me survive only to kill me?

She had to stop. She couldn't take another step. Her legs were made of rubber. She sank to her knees. She looked up at the stars. They were brilliant in the cold, almost frosty air. Her last picture of the world would be a beautiful one, she thought. Her head lowered and she began to cry though no tears fell. She was so tired. Her head was swimming. Stay upright. Her body ignored the command. She toppled over, on the edge of passing out.

She heard footsteps on the trail behind her. She was too weary to open her eyes but the footsteps stopped and she knew someone was standing over her. Had Jules finally caught her? Could he make up that much ground?

She curled protectively into the fetal position.

Suddenly there were two hands reaching underneath her. Then she heard a grunt as a large man straightened up with her cradled in his arms.

I wonder what Burke's first name is, Pauline wondered as she passed out.

24

New York City

PATRICK WHEELER JUMPED THE OILY puddle onto the curb as a cab cut the corner tight, splashing a sheet of filthy water that drenched his pants, socks, and shoes from the knees down.

Jerk!

Wheeler wasn't sure the driver steering the hurtling missile even saw him.

Wind cut through his lightweight jacket. Snow in October? Not quite. The glistening mist that fell through the city lights of the Meatpacking District was only a couple of degrees warmer than full-blown snowflakes. Close enough. The temperature had to have dropped to the thirties. Where was the global warming that the world had been promised since he was a kid? What was the deal with this polar vortex?

Why didn't I wear my heavy coat?

He had a four-block east-west walk to his apartment from the subway station on Canal Street. Four long blocks. It could be worse.

And where was the big career he was supposed to have? He was only twenty-seven, but that was still too old to be sharing an undersized apartment in Manhattan with two roommates. Even if the Meatpacking District was the place to live. His ten by eight bedroom with no window was bad enough, but the apartment had only one bathroom. Sharing a bathroom with two other guys was enough to make long hours as a serf in the empire of KPMG seem preferable to being home. The less time in the suffocating little apartment, the better. There was a reason he went out for a couple drinks almost every night.

He was living in a great part of town and the happening spot to be for his age. In exchange, all he had to surrender was his privacy, dignity, and reasonable access to a shower and toilet.

He did well with his accounting degree from the University of Tennessee in Knoxville. He couldn't wait to finally leave the state. New York, Chicago, San Francisco, and Houston were his preferred destinations. He got his top pick. The Manhattan office.

But he couldn't have graduated at a worse time. The economy was in the dumps. He got the first job easy enough. He had frat brothers who hadn't landed anything for a year or two. But he had expected a lot more. His starting salary was sixty-four thousand dollars, which might have sounded like a lot in his hometown of Winchester, Tennessee, but didn't go far in New York City. He spent two years doing sixty-hour workweeks to pay his dues, but all he had was a small stepping-stone promotion and a raise of ten percent. So he quit KPMG to get an MBA at New York University and improve his marketability. Two years later, the economy was still in recovery. Recovery? Right. The tailspin had hit bottom. So after a couple dozen job interviews—including one with the FBI, which would not be a lucrative a career, but still sounded pretty good to his southern fried patriotism, he hired back with KPMG, just one small stepping stone above square one, with another fifty grand in student loans.

At least he was out of audit and in the consulting division. His next promotion would be a good one.

Keep telling yourself that.

He was tired of waiting.

Time to go back to Knoxville? Give Nashville a try? Something's gotta give.

He keyed himself into the small Spartan lobby of his building, walked past the single elevator, and hoofed it up ten flights of stairs, two steps at a time. He wasn't fat, but he had put on fifteen pounds in the past four years and wasn't exactly thin anymore. He had to start getting more exercise. And start drinking less. Booze was a major reason some of his Sigma Nu brothers had taken longer to enter the workforce.

He passed five doors, fumbled to get his key in the deadbolt, turned the lock, and entered the small common room of his apartment. He stopped in the threshold and stared. Two middle-aged men in dark blue suits were sitting on the couch, looking as if they owned the place. Maybe they did.

"Patrick Wheeler?" one asked as he stood.

"Who is asking?" Patrick asked back, not feeling as confident as he hoped he sounded.

The two men were on their feet and both pulled leather holders from pockets and flipped back the front flaps to reveal shiny badges that said FBI just as clear as day.

I filed my taxes on the simple form. I don't have a car so there isn't a drawer filled with tickets. I haven't had sex with anyone underage because I haven't had sex in months. I pay my student loans on time. I have health insurance. What does the FBI want with me?

"I'm agent Greene and this agent Rasmussen," the man closest to him said.

"Okay."

An awkward pause.

"Uh, what do you need from me?"

"We need a couple hours of your time," Greene said.

"And you came by my apartment to tell me that?"

"Yes, we did."

"I have a phone."

Neither man responded. There was another awkward pause. Wheeler pulled out his iPhone and hit the calendar icon.

"When were you thinking? I'm at client offices all week."

"We need to meet with you right now," Greene said.

"Seriously? Now?"

The two large men didn't feel the need to answer.

"This is crazy," Wheeler said. "You can't expect me to drop everything and just go with you."

"That's exactly what we expect and that's exactly what's going to happen, Patrick," Greene said. "Let's stop wasting time. It is time to roll."

"It's nine o'clock," Wheeler protested. "I just got off work. I have an early start tomorrow."

"I apologize for the inconvenience, Patrick, but we need you now. I should have mentioned, you will be compensated for your time."

"Is this a job interview?" Wheeler asked. "I did put in an app with the FBI but never got a call back."

"I'm not authorized to tell you the exact nature of this meeting," Greene said.

"I can't miss my morning meeting," Wheeler stated with all the bravado he could muster. "This can't go longer than two hours. Tops."

"It'll take two hours if that's all the time we need from you," Greene said. "If it takes longer, that's life."

"I just told you I can't miss my morning meeting."

"You might have to," Agent Greene said. "If that becomes necessary, we'll make appropriate arrangements with your employer."

"They may not take kindly to that," Wheeler said. "We're behind schedule on a big project."

"Don't worry about KPMG, Patrick," Greene said. "They're a big company and can handle your potential absence just fine."

True. But can I?

What was going on?

"Do I have time to grab a bite?"

"We'll have food brought in," Greene said with ill-concealed impatience.

"Do I need to bring anything?"

"We have everything you need," the agent answered. "It's time to roll. Now."

Greene was giving an order, not a suggestion. Did he have a choice? Could the FBI do this? If this was a job interview, there were better ways to make a great first impression.

He did another quick inventory of his boring existence. No fights. No money laundering or fixing books for KPMG clients. No political activity. Nothing. He wasn't being arrested he didn't think, which couldn't always be assumed post-Patriot Act.

Why in the world does the FBI need me? I wish I knew something from the corporate world that would rise to the level of an FBI investigation. Is this a job interview?

"Can I see those badges again?" Wheeler asked, stalling for more time to think.

The two men looked at each shrugged and held out their badges and identification again.

Wheeler shrugged. How would he know if they were legitimate or not?

"Let's get this over with," he said in surrender.

He locked the deadbolt and followed the men toward the elevator.

Greene slid in the backseat next to Wheeler. Rasmussen drove. Greene wasn't impressed. The kid might be smart but he was definitely naïve, he thought. Neither description mattered. That's not why the kid was needed. There was an old saying, it's not what you know that matters most; *it's who you know.* In this case, Wheeler had hit the mother lode with whom he knew. He probably didn't even know it.

Greene and Rasmussen weren't actually in the FBI. Wheeler didn't need to know that either.

25

Los Angeles, California

ZORAIZ, DRESSED IN BLACK ATHLETIC garb from head to toe, stepped from the Navigator with his three companions. Some in his position would resent having to execute the task at hand. It was a job for younger men—men like Fahad at Wonder World—expendable men. But this was a particular mission he savored for himself. He would not miss it for all the fleeting pleasures of the world. If he fell in service to Allah, he would enter Eternity as a martyr. His director would be unhappy that he had to find someone to take his place to handle their West Coast operations—but he would ensure that holy duty was accomplished successfully. The other operations would not be jeopardized if he were dead. He had carefully trained and vetted his young lions and panthers for their assignments. They would not falter.

He cut down a side street, his three lieutenants in tow, to the secluded location he had selected to observe the Islamic Center of West Los Angeles.

His instructions were simple. Let Southern California know the face of true Islam. He had meticulously planned a week of events that could not be ignored. Wonder World was the climax and would strike terror in the general population. What he was about to do would kindle

the embers of fear into a blazing flame in the Muslim population—
the barely-Muslim population, he snorted. So many men and women
who presumptuously claimed the name Muslim—*slave of God*—had
wandered from the faith. This act would announce that comfort and
compromise were no longer acceptable. Turn to Allah in true devotion
and obedience—or die.

Imam Tashbeed Nasif, a professor in the sociology department
at UCLA and a leading moderate voice for peace in the Muslim
community—a *kafir*—a dog who would burn in the deepest pits of
hell—a man who met with Christians and Jews as equals—had been
invited to deliver a speech on bringing peace in a pluralistic culture.

Dog! Whore! Enemy! Kafir! You are no true Muslim.

The main meeting room held 300 seats and was expected to be
filled with Muslims, Christians, Jews, godless atheists, and other
enemies of Allah. How could Nasif even be called an Imam?

A handsome movie star would be present to introduce the Imam.
He was married to a political activist who claimed to be Muslim but
was nothing more than a tool of the West, a follower of Satan.

He nodded and the three others moved to their pre-assigned
places. Timing was everything.

The crowd outside the center was beginning to thin as the time for
Nasif to speak ticked down. He would wait for one particular limo—
the one carrying the handsome movie star and his beautiful wife—
before he gave the signal to move.

Each of the four men carried an Uzi that could discharge 600
rounds in a minute. He didn't like to use anything made in Israel, but it
was the best weapon available for the assault. The men carried enough
magazines to discharge 9mm Parabellum ammo continuously for three
minutes. No one would be left alive. If a few miraculously survived,
that would be fine. They would be shattered witnesses of what happens
to those who betray the Prophet.

The gleaming black Escalade pulled up even with the door. Just a driver. No personal security—they trusted the rent-a-cop agency hired by the Islamic Center. Big mistake on the couple's part. The men in ill-fitting blazers with shield-shaped patches sewn on the chest would pose no problem. One of the men, the supervisor for the evening, in fact, worked for Zoraiz. His job was to know where the other security men were and shoot them if they posed a threat to the assault.

A couple of news stringers shot photos as the actor took his wife's arm to escort her up the steps and into the building.

Now was the time to wait for everyone to be seated.

Zoraiz reached for a cigarette and reminded himself that no matter how anxious and excited he became, he couldn't do anything to reveal his presence. He stuck a piece of gum in his mouth.

After five minutes of shifting from foot to foot and chewing every last trace of flavor from the gum, he saw two flashes of light, the signal from his man inside the conference room. The people were seated. It was show time.

"Move," he hissed into the mouthpiece.

He didn't even look to see if his instructions were being followed. He and one of his men would go through the front door, the other two men through side doors. All were to be unlocked.

Zoraiz began firing in the entrance hall, taking down stragglers who had to make a trip to the bathroom or finish a drink—what had the world come to with an open bar in a supposed center dedicated to Allah? He could hear shots and screams as he entered the back doors of the auditorium.

Two rear exit doors and two side exit doors, each was blocked by an Uzi-wielding attacker. There was nowhere for the crush of people to run, even though the sheep being slaughtered tried vainly to escape, creating a riot of writhing and collapsing humanity. The four men calmly and methodically moved up and down the aisles, blasting bodies in striped motions to make sure no one escaped judgment.

The actor, his wife, and the event organizers were already dead. Only Nasif stood alive on the stage. He stared with hatred at Zoraiz.

"Kafir!" Zoraiz shouted at him.

"Fool!" Nasif bellowed back. "You are so foolish you don't even know what you have done. You bring shame on your faith. You kill your own people and friends of your people. Countless more will die because of your depraved anger. You dishonor the Prophet."

"All I do is for the Prophet. All you do is based on your own honor, your own comfort, your own twisting of the Koran."

Zoraiz was ready to say more, but a single shot exploded from behind him. A red, white, and gray crater erupted in the center of the Imam's forehead. He stayed erect for another two heartbeats, and then crumpled, his head bouncing off the podium as he careened back on top of the handsome movie star.

Zoraiz whirled to see which of his men robbed him of his thunderous honor. It was his man with the security company.

"You must go now. Police are on the way. Go now!" shouted his inside man.

Zoraiz's muscles tensed. His face was a mask of rage. He lifted the Uzi and loosed a staccato barrage of bullets into the man, obliterating his features. Killing him was already a potentiality in order to sever connections to him. But when the man stole his glory and dared order him to move, it was inevitability. Zoraiz prayed that Allah would not look kindly on the man's insubordination.

Paradise is not for such as him.

The three men looked at Zoraiz warily. He nodded and they moved to the back exit quickly.

They were back on the street where the car was parked in three minutes, leaving the bloody, mangled carnage behind them. Sirens wailed as police responded, but they had pulled away from the curb of the scruffy suburban street before the first responder arrived.

That was almost too easy, Zoraiz thought, his eyes gleaming with the last traces of the adrenaline rush.

As Zoraiz pulled to a stop sign, he looked down quickly and hit send on a text that had already been composed: *Job done. Allah be praised.*

Zoraiz drove through a couple of intersections and made two quick turns. He then pulled the Navigator to the curb of the side street he had turned on. He climbed out and dropped the cheap prepaid Nokia cell phone to the ground and used the butt of his Uzi to smash it into a thousand pieces. He kicked the pieces through the grill of the drainage opening to the sanitary sewer. He got back into the SUV and drove away.

He dropped each of the men at his home in silence, thinking about Wonder World and other fireworks he had planned for the sprawling, godless City of Angels.

He hoped his young protégé, Fahad, the Panther, was ready for his assignment.

Zoraiz had big plans for Fahad.

Chicago, Illinois

ALAN JOHNSON WAS AT DINNER with his wife and kids in a crowded restaurant. Feeling the vibration, he glanced down at his phone, read the screen, and smiled. He apologized profusely for using the phone during family dinner and reminded his children that this was bad manners. He dabbed at the corner of his mouth with a white napkin and picked up his fork to finish the mouthwatering piece of carrot cake he ordered for dessert.

If Zoraiz Tariq knew who he was really working for his head would explode. Johnson frowned.

Do I know who I am working for?

26

Boston, Massachusetts

WAITING HAD ALWAYS BEEN ONE of Dr. Rodger Patton's main strengths. You don't become a research scientist if you are impatient. His scientists were still still busy at work, but his job at the moment was to watch and learn from what was about to unfold.

Patton decided to leave the office early—it was only a twelve-hour day—and return to his home on Beacon Hill, where he would go to the basement and release tension on his rowing machine while watching CNN, BBC, and Al Jazeera on the three TV monitors set up to kill the mind-numbing boredom of exercise.

Dr. Rodger Patton, a Ph.D. in cellular and molecular biology from Harvard University, could barely contain his elevated heart rate.

I must exercise.

The first two major beta tests from his laboratory were underway. One was designed to test kill efficacy. The second was designed to disable and distract. Both were designed to create conflict.

He didn't know details of the Patmos military initiatives, but they were designed for the same purposes. From the standpoint of an observer, he was curious if biological or traditional warfare would hold the key to achieving the Patmos goals. With what they hoped—and needed—to accomplish, he didn't care. But still, he couldn't help but cheer for the triumph of applied molecular science.

Disruption of the food supply would be devastating, but would take longer to work. That's what intrigued him so much about the flesh-eating plague led by Dr. Dolzhikov, which was being delivered in the enhanced form created by the work of Dr. Claire Stevens.

The beauty of the Sana'a Ebola test was not the number of evil people it would kill—they were releasing only a whisper of Mariana—Claire Steven's quaint name for the chimera was first scoffed at and then adopted for its charm. It was the number of moderate people it would kill that mattered, moderate being a relative concept in the Middle East. If you bombed a terrorist camp, the entire Islamic world would publically react with anger and calls for revenge. But the vast majority of Muslims would secretly be relieved that radicals were dead. Radicals were as dangerous to them as they were to the West. Of course, terrorists would be replaced by new recruits, but a more immediate danger would be eliminated.

But kill men that minded their own business and caused little to no trouble and the outcry would be widespread and come straight from the heart. It would provoke true emotion and action. Even if the kill ratios in Sana'a were below expectations, he was certain the beta would be a success.

Stevens' enthusiasm for the immediate success of the virus was contagious—no pun intended—and despite misgivings about her petulant temperament, he hoped she was right.

Patton switched off the lights in his office, locked the door, and punched in the security code across from the receptionist's desk before exiting the suite. He took the elevator down to the garage level, mulling over the pluses and minuses of the brilliant and temperamental Claire Stevens.

As he started the engine of his Audi 7, he opted for a Rachmaninov concerto rather than the news. That would make it easier for him to keep rowing to the music of headline news. His commitment to Patmos had come at a physical cost. He was fifty pounds heavier than when he started—and he had already been fifty-pounds overweight at the time. If he was to be at the forefront of building a brave new world, he needed to take better care of his earthly temple in order to savor the fruits of his labors.

In the week or two that the world slowly became aware of the biomedical tragedy unfolding in Sana'a, investigators from a rainbow of countries and agencies would look for answers. Clues planted by Patmos counterintelligence operatives would point them to Al Qaeda, ISIS, the Saudis, the Americans, Kurds, Turks, Russians—always the Russians, such easy targets—the Israelis, the quiet and secretive Swiss, and tribesmen from Saudi Arabia and northern Yemen—all in equal measure. The investigators' work would be an impossible slog through muck and mire as guns and accusations blazed. Guns and accusations their team was augmenting, sometimes paid for by the victims themselves. Brilliant.

Recruiting Dimitri Dolzhikov had been his greatest coup as head of Jonathan Alexander's bioweapons team. Though in his seventies, Dolzhikov was still energetic and brilliant. His specialties in the Soviet Biological Warfare program were Ebola and Marburg. He earned a Ph.D. from the Moscow Institute of Physics and Technology—"the Russian MIT"—at the age of twenty-one, immediately becoming the youngest member of the Russian Academy of Sciences. While at MIPT he was sent to Petrograd State University for specialized study under Nikolay Semyonov, who had been awarded the Nobel Prize in Chemistry in 1956. Semyonov invited Dolzhikov to teach at Petrograd, but the Soviet apparatchik had different plans for him. Back in Moscow, he was teaching doctoral students at Moscow State University at age twenty-two. Most of his brilliant students were four or five years older than him.

By age twenty-four he was immersed in the Soviet bioweapons program. He had seen and done it all, helping the Soviet Empire weaponize and stockpile thirteen different bio-agents, including anthrax, plague, botulism, smallpox, and Marburg.

Dozhikov preferred Marburg over Ebola—something Patton never revealed to Alexander. That ship had sailed. Patton had already spent too much time, money, and energy acquiring the building blocks of an Ebola pandemic—not just for a slice of West Africa that was easily contained and that made grand but safe theater for rock star benefit concerts—but a pandemic that showed the potential of reaching the only place people truly cared about; home. Marburg might be better but there wasn't enough time to change course. Dozhikov agreed Ebola was adequate and nearly as deadly as what he considered to be the clear first choice. The millions of euros he was paid up front and annually certainly helped Dozhikov be flexible.

The world academic community expressed conflicting assessments of Dozhikov's contributions to science when news of his death from a massive stroke hit the international news wires, a necessary red herring.

One of the reasons Patton recruited Claire Stevens was that Dozhikov was a horny old goat who flourished when pretty young women were around. And no question, Claire was a beauty. She was a prima donna that pouted when she didn't get her way, but that made her even prettier. The fact that Stevens had shown true brilliance and initiative with the improved delivery and absorption properties to the Ebola-based chimera was a pleasant surprise and icing on the cake.

Little did she know how close she came to being rejected for the Patmos Lab. She put him in a tough spot by lying about her history of depression. He personally vouched for her, which sealed the appointment and spared her life. Smart people could be so naïve. If she'd been rejected, did she really think they would let her live, knowing as much about them as she did?

But so far her work with Dozhikov and the other lab team members was a stunning success.

Patton was personally heading up the second beta event, which was equally fascinating and potentially more deadly—at least in his mind. A rule of thumb in warfare is that it is usually more effective to disable an enemy population than to kill it. Why? It is far more expensive for your enemy to care for the sick and wounded than bury their dead. What better way to disable the enemy population than striking at the food supply? When the CIA introduced the African swine fever virus into Cuba in 1971, Castro himself had to give the order to slaughter five hundred thousand hogs to stop a nationwide animal epidemic. It was a bad year for Cuban sandwiches. The politically incorrect joke in the world espionage community was that "Fidel didn't bring home the bacon."

When Patton started developing Alexander's bioweapons program he had wanted to work with several invasive plants that would destroy the permaculture of certain targets. But it was impossible to project the rate and extent of spread, which made it impossible to meet Alexander's timetable requirements. Herbicidal cannibalism was still on the back burner for future use as plans unfolded.

Patton turned his research to toxic pesticides as diverse as DDT and Agent Orange. He and his assistants had focused on the worst of the worst from Agent Orange, 2,3,7,8-Tetrachlorodibenzo-p-dioxin, as the basis for their herbivore on steroids.

The next debate was determining the first target.

He personally wanted to hit China's breadbasket, the Shandong Province. China met the criteria of being the most egregious reason the earth's population growth was killing the planet for everyone else—and the government's easing of the one-child law was going to make their role on Earth hitting the Malthusian tipping point even worse. With the number of mouths to feed there, the logistics of delivering the tonnage of unanticipated foreign grain needed if their crop production was cut by even twenty percent would be impossible to execute. Yes, China would be perfect, he thought.

"But delivering the Big Orange will be tough there," one assistant said.

"We can recommend it and let the logistics team tell us it can't be done," Patton responded.

"But why shoot a horse that's already dead?" asked his longtime friend, colleague, and project manager, Bob Jenkins, a brilliant agricultural scientist that hid his killer mind behind a good old Nebraska farm boy persona.

"What do you mean?" Patton had asked him as the other members of the group looked at Bob.

"Our populous neighbors from the Far East have 337 million acres of arable land. Their kind and benevolent government has finally admitted that two percent of that acreage is too polluted to grow crops. And be aware, they aren't acres of land like we have in Nebraska. That's mighty big of them to finally fess up they got a problem. But not big enough. The UN's numbers don't agree with the Chinese numbers and suggest that eight million acres, more than twenty percent of the land, are so filled with carcinogenic metals that any crops grown there will make going hungry feel like a picnic in the park. Heck there's enough cadmium in the soil to put half the population on dialysis.

"Now I love the fine folks at the UN," Jenkins continued, "but everyone in this room knows that some of the UN's official commission reports might fudge things a little this way or that, depending on *whom* they want to pick on or *whom* they want to keep happy. If my French *amie*, the esteemed Dr. Genevieve Mitterand, isn't familiar with the American use of the word 'fudge' in the context of my statement, just think of that feller Pierre who gave you a box of chocolates to prove his love for you, when all along you knew that what he really wanted was to get you in the sack."

Jenkins would have explained the idiomatic background of "in the sack" to the unsmiling Mitterand had Patton not given him an impatient nod and roll of his hand to keep moving.

Nonplussed, Jenkins forged on: "The good folks at the UN get ignored by the Chinese so much they toned the report down so that maybe they'll get along a little better. I guarantee it. And I would know. I think I've personally worn out three pairs of my mighty fine Timberland hiking boots tromping over half them 337 million acres taking samples."

"What are you saying Bob?" Patton had said, interrupting Jenkins' cogent but meandering stream of thought. "What's your point? You're convincing me Shandong is ideal."

"Plenty of time to turn up the heat there, Rodger. As part of the second or third phases of our operations. Unless they do our job for us all by themselves, we can make a bad situation worse. But right now, there are so many variables in what makes the Chinese agricultural system run, and this is my real point, I'm not sure what I'd claim or not claim as our doing when things go bad. We can't control test conditions. We won't be able to project future results when we amp up scalability."

Impossible to argue, Patton thought then and now. Discussion moved from China and the majority of scientists at the table wanted the team to look hard at Central Africa. Jenkins again derailed the train of thought, reminding his colleagues that ironically, famine was such a widespread and perennial condition of the region that the compassionate aid infrastructure was too developed to let their coming disaster kill the number of people they wanted dead. Sure, half the grain intended for famine victims rotted in ports because of the region's brutal politics. But a lot of food would get through. Too much. Too many NGOs and ministries stood ready to defy the warlords and deliver it.

"We've already seen enough prolonging of misery by blocking nature's own plan," Patton said. "I don't think I could stand the disappointment. Where else?"

Jenkins' alternative made immediate sense to everyone at the table. Patton smiled as he thought of Jenkins' surprising proposal.

The Ukraine. Russia's breadbasket. The region was already filled with suspicion and gunfire. It was a powder keg ready to ignite. If not immediately, then as soon as the store shelves in Moscow were empty of bread. Brilliant.

Claire Stevens would have sulked at not getting her way even if she knew an alternative choice was right. Not Patton. Aces in their places. Dr. Robert Jenkins was right. Why hire brilliant people and not listen to them?

Patton broke from his reflections as he steered the Audi onto his block. He was disappointed he had not given Rachmaninov any attention.

I have to give myself some breathing room.

He pulled the sleek automobile into the narrow single car garage. The latest reports he had read earlier that evening—why read again? He nearly had them memorized—gnawed at and twisted his guts. When had he ever experienced such eviscerating impatience? Yes, I need to row. And wait patiently. He thought of their final choice for the mass defoliation of grain beta again.

Patton loosened his belt with a sigh. He tugged down his trousers and threw them on top of his suit coat and shirt. It was too hard to bend over and pull off his socks, so he put his right foot on the heel of his left sock, almost falling when he pried the sock off by lifting his left leg.

I have to lose 100 pounds. I must row. Every day.

The Ukraine it was. What was one more unidentified airplane flying over rolling farmland?

27

New York City

BURKE CONTINUED TO NURSE TONIC water in a highball glass in the Oak Room located in the Plaza Hotel, a wood paneled bar half a flight down on 57th Street, just south of Central Park. He had been there an hour already. This was no time to have a drink and a drink would have to wait until the operation was complete. He would need one. But now he needed a place to wait for Intel without looking like he was loitering. No one knew he was only sipping tonic but the bartender. He needed to fit in. No one knew his exact location except his men on the street, but you could never be too careful.

It didn't help that a middle-aged blonde in a little black dress that revealed long tanned legs below and an ample décolletage above the scoop neck was hitting on him. Again. At least she kept trying to strike up a conversation. He would put her out of her misery and tell her directly that nothing was going to happen between them, but that wouldn't be fitting in. So he laughed and gave quick responses to her incessant banter.

She crowded in a little closer and began to run a finger on top of his hand.

He didn't want this right now. His agent—heck, she was nothing more than an amateur thief and hooker—had shot and uploaded six pictures to him. And just as suddenly she went silent.

Burke spoke three languages fluently and could butcher two more, including Greek. He just wasn't sufficiently versed on the alphabet and grammatical structure Alexander used to trust his immediate translation. Alexander had no formal education, but had come up with what seemed to be a pigeon of modern and Koine Greek in meticulous Cyrillic lettering. What he skimmed over couldn't be what his client expected to glean from Jonathan Alexander's journal. It had nothing to do with business.

He kept coming back to what he could make out. The blood red horse of the apocalypse. The beast. Napoleon. Hitler. Alexander the Great. Western Civilization against the rest of the world. The will to rule. Put it all together and it was a fantasy that conspiracy theorists and theological nuts dreamed of in their arcane contemplations.

It was the stuff of mass genocide. No way. Not even a megalomaniac like Alexander would consider such thoughts. Or would he?

Burke needed to stay focused on what was right in front of him—except the blonde's cleavage and wandering hands that had worked down to the top of his thigh. He had more pressing issues now. Primarily a missing operative. He would confirm a better translation of the opening pages of the journal later.

That's all Pauline transmitted. Then she just stopped. That was more than ten hours ago. No word from her since. A lack of communication would be fine and expected had she not started sending pictures in the first place. He had embedded a number in her smartphone to call if she had questions, needed to share information or was in trouble. The line was picked up by someone who identified himself as a worker at La Bon Bouche patisserie in Luxemburg. Henri was reliable and could handle information and most problems. If it was an emergency situation, Pauline's call would be immediately routed directly into Burke's permanent cell, never used but carefully guarded for one call only, hers, which was always on and always at his side. He switched phones often, but the randomized satellite path from his number would always find where he was and what he was using once he added a program through an app he dubbed Martian Invasion into the new unit. Pauline's instructions had been to make contact only if absolutely necessary. Alexander was a formidable man and knew what was going on around him. She had called only once in the past six months. That was three days ago to let him know she was going to make the move to lift Alexander's journal on their trip to Bentonville.

Bentonville? What the heck was Alexander doing in Bentonville? Was he planning to take control of Walmart, the largest company in the world? Retail didn't seem like his style. But who knows?

Until he got Pauline in Alexander's camp, it had been nearly impossible to follow the man. It was his second month on the assignment when it dawned on him that Alexander had a double. It wasn't hard to figure out after that when Alexander wanted to keep his whereabouts a secret. His double would show up at his estate on the French Riviera or his ranch in Argentina.

His mind traveled back to Pauline. What had happened? Burke hoped it was a simple matter that she had heard someone coming—probably the human killing machine named Jules—and had aborted before being exposed. She would return the journal where she found it and wait for a better time to finish. But he knew that was wishful thinking. Alexander's Gulfstream left Bentonville and landed at the Teterboro Airport in New Jersey two hours ago. His watcher confirmed what he already knew in his heart. Pauline didn't get off the plane. Neither did Jules. What more evidence did he need that her cover was blown and she was somewhere being questioned or already dead? For the first time in a violent career spent among the worst the world had to offer, he had failed. He had not delivered Alexander's journal to his client.

Burke had lost operatives before. Two to be exact. But both men were professional dogs of war that fully understood the risk-reward nature of the business. Pauline wasn't professional. He first saw her in the lobby bar of the Hostel Hassler at the top of the Spanish Steps in Rome. She was the escort on the arm of an Italian businessman. So technically, she was a professional. Burke had just finished a job for the Director General of the Gendarmerie Corps of the Vatican City State. The Catholic Church was being blackmailed by a con artist from Boston, Massachusetts. Burke delivered a report—an expensive report—that capped the Vatican's liability to his fees and an already hefty legal bill. But not the multi-million-dollar settlement the man Burke exposed was seeking.

The Italian businessman drank heavily and began to get loud and aggressive. When Pauline didn't respond the way he wanted to one of his crude jokes he slapped her on the face. Burke was old school Middle America. A man doesn't hit a woman—unless she pulls a gun on him first, which had happened to Burke on more than one occasion. He still had never struck a woman.

Burke acted quickly. He walked over to the man and using only his forefinger gave a quick, sharp tap to the notch above the man's sternum, just below the throat. A level three pressure point, it was not intended to cause pain or permanent damage. But the love tap created an immediate and powerful gag reflex—it's tough to be a tough guy when you feel like you are about to vomit—followed by queasiness, and then what felt like an involuntary step—or flop—backward, which was his desired effect. This trick always worked for Burke. Even the most belligerent combatant backed off. The other reason it was one of his favorite nonlethal moves was that it usually went completely unnoticed. If someone did see his finger dart forward, it would appear to be nothing more than some angry finger wagging, with maybe a little poke to the chest. Nothing to get too concerned about. Mind your own business.

The man sat down with a stunned but docile expression. He probably didn't realize how lucky he was. Burke wanted to punch him in the nose with the base of his palm to hear cartilage and bone crunch. But he restrained himself.

Pauline took his proffered arm and they headed down the Via Margutta, a popular side street off the Piazza de Spagna. After a brisk silent walk, they settled in the lobby of the Hotel Manfredi. He asked if she would like to have dinner with him and she said she would be delighted to. They spoke in French until one in the morning. She was charmed that an American could be so fluent in her native tongue. Okay, she knows how to flatter a man's ego, Burke had recognized.

During their conversation, he learned about her childhood in a home with two alcoholics. He liked that she was honest and direct about her life since age sixteen. She didn't euphemize what she did for a living, nor did she apologize or glamorize. She didn't blame. She owned what she had become and took responsibility for her life. She didn't whine that she had only received half her fee for her time with the Italian businessman. She let Burke know that she was looking for a way out of the business.

Burke felt he was a good judge of people and he believed her. He hoped it wasn't just because she was so beautiful. Oh, was she beautiful.

Burke was attracted to her but unexpectedly felt a pang of his long lost sense of honor and morality. He registered a room for her at the Manfredi and told her to get checked in. Then he went back to the Hassler, picked the lock to her room, and packed her suitcase while the Italian businessman cursed and threatened him in at least five languages. But he never left the velvet loveseat after Burke ordered him to sit and not move. The man still looked a little squeamish.

Burke delivered her luggage to the front desk of the Manfredi, arranged transportation to the airport in the morning for her, and left a confirmation number for a first class seat to Luxemburg. He paid for everything.

He wasn't sure he would ever talk to Pauline again, but he kept her number. He wanted to connect with her a number of times in the year that followed but could never bring himself to make contact. In his world you didn't purposely pursue entanglements and complications. But then he needed her to help him set the honey trap for Alexander. It was not lost on him that she could pass for a twenties version of Alexander's wife, Helena. He called to set up a meeting time.

The negotiation for her services was painful. He sensed that maybe she had thought of him over the past year as well and was hoping the purpose of his call was for a different, less tainted reason. Again, he might think that she had real feelings for him because he wanted to believe it, creating a false sense of guilt. Whether or not that was the case, he was not proud of himself for what he was asking her to do.

You have a strange way of telling a girl you like her, Burke said to himself. What in the world happened to you?

But they agreed to a deal. It was her means to a new life. It was the highest subcontractor fee he had ever paid. Two million euros. He wondered if Pauline and he could start over after the operation and see each other with fresh eyes. Doubtful. By enlisting her as a high priced escort he had closed that door. What was he supposed to say? I know that I used to be your pimp, but believe me, all I ever wanted was to get to know you better. He shook his head in disgust.

It was an outrageous idea to connect with someone after being disjointed so emphatically by what he had asked her to do. He wasn't sure what the road back to normal human interaction would be for him with her or anyone else.

"You look preoccupied, darling," the blonde said. "Can I help take your mind off something?"

"I'm not sure there's any chance of that, but thank you for the offer."

"Was that an offer I just made?"

"Pardon me. I was presumptuous."

She laughed. "Of course it was an offer. A standing offer. I've been told I can be very helpful. Was it a woman who hurt you? We can be such bitches."

"I'm sure you know how to help me, but not tonight."

She looked hurt.

"Let me buy you a drink," Burke said.

"Get another one for yourself and maybe you'll change your mind," she said with a pouty expression that was overridden by a twinkle in her eyes.

He caught the bartender's eye and pointed at both glasses.

He had a man watching Alexander's townhome and another sitting at the bar in Per Se down the street. Why? Pauline wasn't on the return flight with Alexander. Face it. She had been caught and had been taken somewhere private and impossible to find for some excruciatingly painful questioning. Or she was already dead. Simple as that. It was his fault.

Burke looked at his phone again. Nothing.

"You really aren't talkative, sweetheart. She must have done a real number on you."

He had almost forgotten about the blonde, impossible as she was making that. He shook his head no and confirmed the answer to her question by saying nothing. This was obviously his cue to leave. He was past trying to pretend to fit in as a lonely heart looking for a pickup. He pulled a hundred from his wallet and put it on the bar as the drinks arrived.

He decided to check on his men working the street and then head back to Harlem.

"Aren't you even going to say goodbye?" the blonde asked to his back.

Nope. I'm not.

There would be no extraction from Per Se, a restaurant on Columbus Circle and one of the City's finest. He already knew Alexander had cancelled dinner reservations. There would be no snatching her off the street in front of Alexander's townhome on 67th Street. She didn't walk off the plane. She wasn't in the City.

Why did I involve her in this? Why didn't I call her when I wanted to get to know her for her own sake?

He walked out the door, ready to disappear into the night.

The blonde watched him exit, picked up her phone, and made a call.

28

Devil's Den Hiking Trail, the Ozark National Forest

THE SWISS ARE FAMED FOR luxury goods, secretive banks, expensive watches, chocolates, political neutrality, and Swiss Army knives. Despite the ubiquitous red acetate butyrate casing that houses magnifying glasses, toothpicks, saws, screwdrivers, and a host of other tools, including the promised knife, the namesake Swiss Army does not command the same international reputation as the knife, primarily because the Swiss Army does not take part in armed conflicts on foreign soil.

Despite being best known for making expensive timepieces, the Swiss do take their military seriously. Ninety-five percent of their armed forces are conscripts who function as the world's largest militia per capita. At the end of two years of active service, all soldiers keep their weapons and military equipment at home—subject to unannounced inspection—as part of their agreement to continue serving in the militia.

At age eighteen, all Swiss males found physically and emotionally fit for service are drafted into the military and spend half a year in training and up to another eighteen months in active service. In rare cases, when all forms of national military service are exempted, the male citizen pays an extra three percent in federal taxes until age thirty. When a national referendum to abolish the draft came to vote in 2013, it was devastatingly defeated with seventy-three percent of voters indicating they believed it was best to keep the draft in place.

Jules did his two years of military service, excelled, and started down a professional career track in the army. He ultimately found the Swiss Army experience to be too inactive. What was the point of learning a craft but never actually doing it?

Jules was a man at sea after the debacle with being rejected by the Swiss Guard. He wondered if the mysterious and brutal murder of the Bishop of Basel could ever be linked to him. Not a chance.

Based on a tip from a friend, he used all the money he had saved and traveled to Fairfax, Virginia. He didn't have an appointment, but after a human resources specialist made time to meet with him, he was hired immediately after he blew away the physical by DynCorp, a private military company. He had found a temporary home. DynCorp did contract work for various governments in exotic destinations like Bosnia, Afghanistan, and Iraq, ostensibly to do security work, but routinely—and off the books—to take part in armed combat on foreign soil.

He still didn't know how Alexander found him, but the great man reached out to Jules through a firm that recruited security professionals. Nothing was ever said, but it was clear that Mr. Alexander desired the services of someone comfortable in both reactive and proactive defense roles. The employer and employee found a match made in heaven—or hell, depending on one's point of view.

At the moment Jules appeared as impassive as a rock in the eyes of the men who were conducting a two-headed search for Pauline—boots on the ground and drones in the air. But inside his emotions were roiling between rage and shame.

When he knew he'd lost Pauline, he returned to the place he first spotted her, removed the silencer from his Sig Sauer P220, and holstered the weapon. He knelt down and gently placed Mr. Alexander's leather portfolio and Pauline's smartphone and fanny pack in a leather shoulder satchel. Her driver had been dismissed and been told Pauline wanted to spend the day walking the trail instead of running it. He told Mr. Alexander's driver a different story, that she wasn't feeling well and wanted to return to the plane. He needed both men out of the area immediately, but telling two stories was just one of his mistakes this trip. At some point the two men would talk and notice the discrepancy.

Mr. Alexander had given him his marching orders to eliminate the discrepancy. Only one man had to die, unless it was determined they had spoken to each other and possibly compared notes.

He worked with Klaus to get a search team on the ground within a few hours. He let Mr. Alexander know he needed to stay and coordinate the hunt. Alexander agreed immediately. A first. Alexander liked Jules close to his side. His rage burned brighter at the thought the man might turn elsewhere for protection.

Has he written me off? Is he looking for my replacement? All I can do is regain his trust.

Jules realized his biggest mistake was the fact that Pauline was still part of Alexander's world. The boss hadn't wanted to listen to him when he expressed concerns about her. He should have made himself heard. That's what a good soldier does. Jules didn't think Alexander was losing his keen ruthlessness—both hideous and beautiful to behold—but he knew big things were underway and there is only so much one man can keep in his sight lines. That's why he was needed. Whether ascribed by Alexander or not, Jules determined to take full responsibility not only for bungling her capture, but also for allowing an enemy inside the camp.

Unacceptable.

She was wounded. She had no known way to communicate to the outside world and call for help. If she did, the team already had a man in Arkansas law enforcement who would alert them to her whereabouts. She was in the middle of a state park—or maybe the National Forest by now—that had no commercial or residential development for miles.

They needed to find her, dead or alive. Both options were preferable to the debilitating state of not knowing.

If they found her dead, he would bury her in the Ozark Mountains—and keep a single eyeball, tooth, and fingertip to add to his collection. Men brought souvenirs of war home with them. Why should his needs be different even if he didn't wear a uniform anymore?

He swore in his mind again that he would personally punish whoever was responsible for this affront. Anything done against Mr. Alexander was an act against Jules.

He hadn't slept for nearly twenty-four hours. That didn't matter. A soldier sleeps when he can and stays awake as long as it takes to kill and not be killed.

There was nothing more he could do to assist in the search. It was time to pay a visit on a professional driver who watched too closely and asked too many questions. He would then drive up the highway to Bentonville to take care of Garrison.

29

New York City

"JONTO! RELAX. THIS IS NOTHING more than a minor setback," a voice with a thick accent said over the phone. Despite his jocularity, the caller was nervous. How was he to know the man was writing something of import in his journal?

Alexander's look was impassive. He said nothing into the phone line. He and Nicky were in the office of his Upper Eastside townhome.

Nicky sat across from him—dark, handsome, patient, loyal, and deadly. He had just reported on his time in the Saudi Peninsula. Something was going right. His boy had done well. Good kid, even if he wasn't a kid anymore—he had worked for him for almost twenty years.

Nicky had been a blur of activity on his chartered flight from Cairo and once he hit the ground. He ordered Jules off the hunt for Pauline to take care of other pressing matters. He dispatched trusted men from Geneva to Luxemburg. He quickly set up a defensive network around the townhome. He gave explicit directions on how Pauline's recovered phone was to be handled.

Maybe the boy is ready to assume executive duties.

Nicky's father and Alexander's older brother, Nikolai, wanted little Nicky to be everything he wasn't, especially legitimate. Alexander was happy to support his brother's wishes. He paid his nephew's way to London School of Economics—it cost almost as much to get him admitted as it did to pay for the hefty tuition. Nicky showed great promise at the LSE—just not as a student. Street work was in his blood, just as obviously as legitimacy ran through the blood of Alexander's own son. Nicky hustled the proven ways to make money on the wrong side of the law while in London: girls, guns, and gambling. Alexander's machine got Nicky out of there in one piece, with no arrest record and a shiny diploma from LSE.

Alexander tried to reason with his brother that there were better ways to employ Nicky's gifts, but the man would not be moved. So Alexander moved Nicky from position to position in his vast network of companies, keeping a close eye to see if there was a perfect match. To his brother's grave disappointment, there wasn't. Except on the side of the law the two brothers had scrabbled up, Nikolai with many slips and stumbles along the way, Jonathan—Jonto—a sure-footed irresistible force. More often than not, brother Nikolai heeded the siren call that had shipwrecked their father. The bottle. Didn't matter if it was ouzo, vodka, wine, moonshine or Japanese whiskey. One innocent sip always led to the entire bottle.

His father's way was not for Nicky. It wasn't that he was lazy. He was a disciplined worker—as long as the work wasn't based in an office and as long as it involved guns, knives, fists, fast cars, secrecy, coercion, evasion, and a late night rendezvous with a beautiful woman as a cherry on the top.

Alexander was not unsympathetic of his brother's plight. After all, his own son wasn't wired the same way as his father either. Along with his wife, Alexander loved his son as much as he could love anyone. He wasn't disappointed—maybe a little relieved—that he picked up his mother's basic goodness with none of his own ruthlessness. He was the son his brother Nikolai had wanted so desperately.

Alexander knew he had to protect both himself and his son, so when he sent Jonathan Jr. to the Wharton Business School at the

University of Pennsylvania, it was with a new and perfectly legal name, Jason Anderson.

To the world, Alexander's son, Jonathan Jr., Johnny, was dead. That took some delicate work in the aftermath of the car crash that had stolen the beauty and mind of his beloved wife, Helena, a one-time model and B-level European film actress. Alexander didn't flinch when called to the scene of the wreckage, but instantly saw and seized the opportunity to protect his progeny. He put an iron curtain around the crash site outside of Nice, France. The first responder, a public servant of modest means, had a daughter who was of university age and he was easily motivated to assist. Other bribes were paid to allow Alexander's hastily assembled technical team to investigate and report on the tragic accident.

Helena, I would have granted you freedom to pursue another life. You didn't have to do what you did.

It took Klaus less than 24 hours to find a body to play the role of young Jonathan. A teenager had crashed a BMW racing motorbike weeks earlier. His parents were already close to pulling the plugs on the life support that was maintaining his vegetative state. It was not hard to provide an inducement to do the inevitable. With gentle maneuvering, the boy was declared dead, his body sent to a crematorium. What the technician on duty put into the ovens Alexander didn't know or want to know. He sincerely hoped the parents believed the ashes in the urn were the remains of their son.

The young man's actual body was described in detail as part of the accident report.

The world press wrote moving accounts of Alexander's great tragedy; his son dead and his wife in a near comatose state.

Alexander hastily secreted Jonathan Jr. to the one place no one but a few trusted advisors knew about; the Isle of Patmos. Birthplace of his own father. Alexander dreaded the conversation with Jonathan Jr. to let him know the mechanizations he put in place that would force him to embrace a new identity. The talk went surprisingly well. Helena had not kept her husband's brutal past nor present as a secret from their son. He jumped at the opportunity to become a new man, set apart from the shadow of his father.

Did that hurt? Of course. But Alexander knew that greatness—immortality—required profound sacrifices.

Loss was also something he was acquainted with from his earliest days. He and Nikolai were actually half brothers—some people found even that hard to believe with Nikolai's tangled shock of black hair and Roman nose in contrast to Jonathan's thin nose and fair features that he inherited from his mother. No two brothers could look less alike.

Nikolai's mom had died in childbirth. A year later, a nineteen-year old French beauty had fallen for the dark, swarthy Greek fisherman she met in a harbor café in the city of Skiathos. She and the boys' father embarked on a passionate love affair that spawned Jonathan. After Jonto's birth, his father resolved again to quit the bottle, which made him a raging bear to live with in contrast to his gentle drunkenness. His mother had enough sooner than later and was gone before Alexander reached his second birthday. All that remained of her for Alexander was a faded photograph on the day she and his father had posed with him for his baptism.

After the faked death, Alexander still saw his son once a year at great risk to the plan. The reason was simple. Johnny loved his mother deeply. That was not the only reason, but it was a substantial reason Alexander spared no expense to keep Helena's shattered earthly existence as comfortable as possible, with a 24-hour team to tend to her every need. He brought the music and art to the house that he knew she loved. When back at the estate outside of Geneva, he would sip a small glass of brandy and hold her hand each evening. It was the closest he ever felt to her or anyone else, even if she tensed at his touch. It didn't hurt that his ministrations as doting husband were some of the few ways that scored points for him in the court of public opinion.

He actually didn't care what the public thought of him but a reasonably positive impression was good for business.

Alexander had never been faithful to his wife, but what people in his inner circle knew was he sincerely loved once-beautiful Helena dearly.

Once a year Klaus would arrange a maze of clandestine travel arrangements to bring Johnny—Jason Anderson—to Switzerland to hold his mother's hand and engage in stilted conversations with his father. Never in the open air where prying eyes in the sky could witness the return from the dead of the son.

At all other times his son was Jason, a successful young man who had lost his parents as a child. Jason had done okay as an investment banker. Nothing earthshattering, but nothing to be ashamed of as a father. He earned an MBA from New York University after Lehman Brothers, his employer, died in the crash of 2008. Alexander tried to warn him but Johnny didn't listen to him.

Alexander often wondered why Johnny hadn't gotten married yet.

"Young men wait these days," his nephew Nicky would say to him. "What's the hurry? There's a lot of options to explore.

Nicky was married with four kids but kept his options open. That worried Alexander a bit, but realistically, he understood Nicky would always need the challenge of a new conquest.

Alexander's own nightly visits with Helena never wavered, even as her mental condition worsened. Helena was and would be the only love of Jonathan's life. Some days she knew her husband, but more days she didn't. Those were the best. To move forward in life, some things are better forgotten, including a mother who deserted him as an infant.

The man on the phone, a most unlikely ally, knew he had pushed his longtime friend too far by calling him by his childhood name of Jonto. He knew that was the least of his worries. He plunged into the awkward silence, saying, "I am working to contain the situation from multiple angles."

"A situation you created."

"What choice did I have? We have carefully cultivated our mutual animosity and loathing of each other for both public and private consumption. Not participating would have thrown that into question."

"But you did not contact me."

"You were the one who put a moratorium on communicating with each other as events approach."

"I would have made an exception had I known you were hiring mercenaries to infiltrate me."

"But look how little was discovered. I had confidence in your defenses and it was well placed confidence."

"Words, important words, I committed to paper have been revealed."

"But what do they mean? They will confuse our enemies more than provide clarity to what is unfolding. Your secret—*our secret*—is safe."

"I only have your word on that, which doesn't reassure me at the moment."

The man on the other end of the line wanted to say Jonto, but caught himself and answered, "Jonathan, it hurts to hear you question my commitment and loyalty to the cause—and to you, the author of our cause. How long have we been friends? Who can you trust more than me?"

Alexander looked at Nicky. Nicky scowled and moved his head from side to side, slowly.

"I'm sure no one," Alexander said with a wink at his nephew who was listening intently to the conversation. "And I'm sure you will prove yourself. This is a minor setback. All the more reason to be more vigilant than ever."

"Is that even possible with you, my friend? I know no one more vigilant than you."

"Apparently more vigilance is possible. For someone was placed close to me."

"And still got nothing."

"Not true. Eleven private handwritten pages is very much something."

"But nothing detailed. Nothing incriminating. The simple musings of a man on the state of the world. No intent was expressed to pursue a course of action."

That part was not quite true.

I should have waited to begin my writing. Now it puts Patmos at even greater risk. It makes me look foolish.

Alexander broke the silence diplomatically: "I am sure you are right, but even so, this is not good. You know the agents placed against me. I want to trust you, but I want you to prove your trust. After all, my friend, you have everything to lose if you have stirred a hornet's nest that cannot be contained."

"Jonathan. Jonathan. Trust me. First of all—and please don't take this as disrespect—I had no idea that there was anything to find. I would never do anything to harm you and the work you have undertaken. As you said, I have as much to lose as you do. I will nip this in the bud. Even as we speak, the operatives are being hunted and will soon face termination. With the few who might read the words, I will bring insight into the writings that cast them in a different light. Your trust shall be rewarded."

"Make it so. With the Middle East so volatile, who knows how America's only assured ally in the region might be deleteriously impacted."

The threat to the country the man loved was palpable.

Why in the hell did Alexander write down that he was the Beast of the Apocalypse? It's been years since we've met in person. Is he losing his marbles? Are the rumors of a stroke true? "I will be the Beast"?

Alexander pushed a button to disconnect the secure line. He hated to use telephones, though each of his residences had a separate connection that sent encrypted calls through a series of switches and

RISE OF THE BEAST

relays that were impossible to follow. Supposedly impossible. The technological geeks will truly rule the world if I don't, he thought.

He looked at Nicky and shook his head. Trust his caller? Never. The man played every angle. No. Alexander didn't trust him. He trusted no one. There was no benefit in it. Not Klaus who organized his life and knew all his secrets. Not Jules who would put his body in front of a bullet for him. Not Patton who headed up the scientific aspects of Patmos. Not even Nicky, soon to be anointed as his second in command, who was blood. He mostly trusted Nicky—though his disloyalty to his wife and children might indicate a willingness to betray others he loved, namely his uncle. So he would not trust even Nicky totally. Besides, when in history had blood proven to be failsafe? History was littered with patricide, filicide, and fratricide. So no, he would never totally trust anyone, including Nicky, who was heading up the more violent operations of Patmos.

Always best to keep another set of eyes on those guarding you.

30

New York City

BURKE WAS GROWING MORE WORRIED by the second. None of his street soldiers were at their posts. What was going on?

He cut over to the Peninsula Hotel and headed to the rooftop bar. Using a pair of military quality Bushnell binoculars, he could spot two of his watch points. No one on duty. He didn't have an angle to check other Jonathan Alexander chokepoints he was monitoring.

What next? Burke wanted to attack. But Alexander would be on high alert and had probably set up defenses accordingly, even if his psychopathic bodyguard was not with him. It would be a quixotic suicide.

It grated at him that with his failure in Northwest Arkansas, he was now running blind. He had no actionable Intel.

What of his street soldiers? No chance they had a simultaneous call from nature and headed for the comfort of inside plumbing. Watchers didn't worry about misdemeanor tickets for public urination.

Were they captured? Most would not be taken without a fight. Dead?

He had succumbed to the biblical sins of pride and greed, Burke thought ruefully. Others were paying the price for his reckless hubris.

He needed to get back to Europe and reconnoiter with Henri. The two of them would come up with a meticulous plan to hit the man hard, possibly with a long-range sniper rifle. No way would he get paid for a blotched assignment, but going after Alexander was no longer a matter of money.

Time to move. Better to be the hunter than the hunted.

31

New York City

THERE ARE SOME THINGS THAT can't be said out loud. So Jonathan Alexander wrote them down, slowly and carefully, using classic lettering that wasn't taught in modern Greek schools. The words were his secrets. He planned for them to be revealed in the light of day sometime in the distant future. But not now. Only at his death so that his name would never be forgotten, thus insuring his immortality.

Alexander reached in the pocket of his lightweight coat and pulled out one of the few tokens he still possessed going back to his childhood. A switchblade. His father had given it to him. He touched the well-worn lever and the blade popped out. He closed it but kept it in his hand. His fingers traced the groove on the side of his head.

No, now was probably not the time to have committed words to a journal. He had not written anything that made him criminally liable or anything that would reveal the extent and specifics of his plans. But anyone reading his journal could portray him as a deranged, crazy chauvinist, undoing the forty years he had carefully cultivated a public persona of refinement after climbing from the treacherous docks of Marseilles, Istanbul, Naples, and Gioia Tauro, along with countless Balkan and Turkish overland routes that supplied the drug trade, the source of his swift rise to wealth.

Alexander flicked open the knife. His fingernails were perfectly manicured but he could not resist the muscle memory of using the blade to clean the dirt, grime, and blood that oozed into the pores and lines of a fisherman's hands.

Alexander had always been subject to rumors about his past and present that claimed he was a sociopathic megalomaniac who would do absolutely anything to get what he wanted. The volume of stories had grown exponentially in the Internet age. Many of those rumors were actually fairly accurate, even if the specifics were often wrong. He had a publicist who was quick to point out that the Internet was an unregulated realm where people could make spurious accusations with no accountability—and thus was not taken seriously.

"Besides, with a man like you, there is no such thing as bad publicity."

That's not what he wanted to hear so she shut up and got back to her job to make sure his charitable acts were well reported by the international press.

Yes, there is such a thing as bad publicity.

If people read his words in his own handwriting that would be bad publicity. Hard, much harder to deny. The public relations team would claim that anything displayed in the media was a forgery and hoax. She had well-compensated sources throughout the press who would give her a heads up if something big and negative about Alexander was about to be published or aired. She would immediately contact Klaus. Alexander's legal team would move quickly to issue cease and desist orders that threatened massive lawsuits that would cause pause for even the most powerful of media conglomerates. But there were too many outlets to ensure everything was stopped. Who knows what would catch fire?

His journal would.

Patmos was using this dynamic of the World Wide Web to help accomplish his plans. But he didn't want the same dynamic used against himself.

He and Nicky were alone on the balcony outside the private office in his Manhattan townhouse, a bottle of wine between them, only half empty. Nicky smoked a Cuban cigar. Alexander thought it was a nasty habit, but he could think of worse substances for Nicky to indulge in—all of which his nephew eschewed under Alexander's watchful gaze—so he paid it no heed. Uncle and nephew were comfortable with silence.

Much had been done in the previous 24 hours. More was undone.

Alexander's mind wrestled with a series of problems that had arisen at precisely the wrong moment. Pauline was wounded and at large. A particularly despicable man, Colonel Arnold Grayson, who had been hired to infiltrate him was also at large. Who knew how many others Grayson involved in the subterfuge? Who had actually seen the pages of his journal? Based on that, who would come after Alexander next?

He had moles in a vast array of governments and corporations worldwide. What did he tell them to look for without revealing too much?

If there were leaks, could he trust the key co-conspirators in the Patmos machination? One of the brethren called him to let him know of his "innocent" involvement in the heist of pages from his journal. The man didn't have to say what Alexander knew was on his mind.

I didn't think you would be foolish enough to write anything down.

The man who called him was a religious man yet failed to grasp the need for a connection to the divine in an undertaking that meant life or death for all that was good and honorable in a world of unremitting misery and thralldom.

What of the other chosen associates he had cultivated and brought into the plan or as much of the plan as he wanted them to know? Did he reach out now to tell them there was a potential problem? If they knew there were new risks, would their commitment and resolve hold? Not every powerful man had the iron will to rule, which was a major reason Patmos was so important. In a world of fantasy and flames, someone had to be the grownup and rule.

Yes, he would reach out to his brothers. He needed them. When he no longer needed them, he would then judge their commitment and deeds before determining their fate in a new world order. Those who did not measure up would be dispatched. He was certain which man would be the first to die.

"Jonto, how was I to know?"

He wondered if any would truly be found worthy. It still chafed that he had to spin such elaborate stories of a new Illuminati, the enlightened few that controlled events from a shroud of invisibility. Why did people need such fanciful notions? Why did lesser men want their names surreptitiously associated with the Grove? The Bilderberg Group? The 32nd Degree Masons? A secret consortium of Central Bankers? Yes, they all held the necessary positions and wealth to exercise power to advance Patmos, but did they possess the true substance to see it to completion? Were they the true descendants of the Illuminati?

Of course not. Alexander knew too well that whatever power a father bequeathed to his son, not every son was capable of donning a mantle that required iron will.

The original Illuminati was historical fact. Jacob Frank was a disciple of the 17th Century occultist, Sabbati Zevi, the man who codified a plan to undermine power structures through chaos. When Frank, Adam Weishaupt, and Mayer Amshel Rothschild founded the Order of the Illuminati in 1776, it was the energy that rallied disparate power brokers to topple the French monarchy. The men infiltrated the highest levels of Judaism, Christianity, Islam, the Scottish Masons, and countless governments. Weishaupt's writings continued to dominate and guide the thinking of many secret societies in the centuries to follow. But there was no contiguous ruling cabal, even if many heirs to the original triumvirate believed themselves to be puppet masters in a shadow government that controlled and profited from both sides of every significant world conflict.

Even if the name and ideals lived on, Alexander was certain that no extant organization existed that had the means to create the disorder required to build a new world order. If a man attended a meeting of the Bilderbergs or the Grove, it was a sure sign to Alexander that he was a mere poseur.

Greatness simply wasn't a byproduct of heredity or wealth.

Alexander would continue to feed their egos, letting them believe they pulled the strings of world events.

The problem with the teachings of Weishaupt was that he was a man of his times, which made his vision myopic. He sought to dissipate the control of Western powers, never factoring in emerging demographic realities. Those who followed his rules were equally near-sighted. What good was it to control the mechanizations of a dying carcass? The savages of the world were the new world order. It was a simple numbers game. Rockefeller's Club of Rome brought population control to the forefront, but again, missed the point by assigning nearly equal desired cuts across the board, rather than focusing on the wastelands of human existence. He, Jonathan Alexander, would not make the same mistake in his plans. The West must rise from the ashes of decay to reassert its world hegemony. The only way that was possible was that much of the world must die.

Alexander thought of his journal again. Would he have done anything differently? How could he? First, there was the question of his own immortality. His name must be spoken through eternity. Second, if there was a God, Alexander must have him on his side or bend him to his will. He knew that God had allowed Lucifer freedom of rebellion throughout history. Alexander was convinced God had a blind spot in regard to the most beautiful being of His creation. Alexander would use that. Had not the Beast prevailed against God countless times throughout history?

He, Alexander, knew without a doubt he must be the man to cleanse the world of unrighteousness, with or without God.

No, he would have done nothing differently. The words had to be written for posterity sake.

He thought back to the second he reached for the journal on the steps of Reverend Garrison's church and discovered it was missing from his vest pocket. He knew in a flash it was Pauline's doing. Jules had warned him of her. That he would do differently. He should have listened. But he liked her. And yes, she carried a remarkable semblance to the young Helena he had fallen in love with. Both were difficult to control, which was both alluring and inconvenient.

"GET SOME SLEEP, UNCLE," NICKY said.

Sleep was difficult. Alexander felt restless. He liked to keep Jules near him, particularly in foreign situations. He knew he was well protected but still felt uneasy.

He had no choice but to dispatch Jules to find Pauline and the journal. Jules was successful in retrieving the journal and her phone, which was helpful, even if he failed to capture the girl.

The phone was rushed to Klaus in Geneva where a trusted technical specialist awaited its arrival. She tore it apart and quickly found the invisible app that forwarded the pictures Pauline took. The woman determined that Pauline had sent only six images. That would equate to between six and eleven pages. Those pages were in someone's possession. And that someone was a threat to him and his plans.

What form would this threat take? Most obvious, if whoever read the journal pages correctly interpreted the words to mean that Alexander had plans to strategically eliminate a sizeable portion of the world's population, he could provide that information to governmental authorities to investigate. Alexander's Patmos activities were laundered through a myriad of corporations, none of them linked to him. But that didn't mean the brightest minds with unlimited resources couldn't connect the dots.

Even if he was too well insulated from being implicated in events that were about to unfold, the plans themselves might be discovered under intense scrutiny. That would be catastrophic. He cared about the plans themselves. Deeply. Almost as much as he cared for himself.

A second form the threat might take, extortion, would be preferable to him. He would of course agree to pay anything on any terms when the demand for money came. But the blackmailer would make the ultimate payment. Painfully. Alexander would spend whatever it took to make it so.

But something else teased at him. Whoever had hired Pauline to photograph the pages of his journal had to be someone he knew and someone who knew him. How else would they know about the journal and become curious about what it contained?

Was it someone that worked for him? Klaus was digging deep into the activities of his top lieutenants this very moment, while one of those lieutenants was digging deeply into Klaus's every activity.

Some would be daunted or discouraged by the task of looking under every rock for an enemy. Not Alexander. What he had Klaus doing was absolutely necessary. But he also knew that among all his enemies, one man stood above. He was not easy to get to, but it helped that one of the man's most trusted friends was also on Alexander's payroll.

Alexander pursed his lips and thought. He appreciated Jules' attempt to take the blame for the Pauline fiasco when he called to let him know the driver had suffered a massive heart attack. That was kind of Jules to care about his feelings and thusly show his loyalty. But it also bothered him; even angered him. When had he ever needed coddling or encouragement? He had performed everything Jules had with his own bare hands long before Jules was but a gleam in his parents' eyes.

Did Jules perceive that he had become soft? Had he become soft at the precise time he needed to be hard? Was the introspection of Patmos dulling the edge of his blade?

"Nicky, am I as strong as I used to be?"

"I think you're stronger than ever."

"Then why did I let an enemy inside my home?"

"You couldn't have known. She was looked at from every angle. She was clean. There was nothing suspicious about her."

RISE OF THE BEAST

"Who introduced her to us?"

"I don't know. Klaus handles that stuff."

"Indeed."

Nicky took a long draw on his cigar, let the smoke linger in his mouth without inhaling, and blew it out slowly, waiting for his uncle to speak again.

"Nicky, what if I told you I think we have a traitor in our midst?"

Nicky took another long pull on the cigar, then answered, "It would both surprise me and not surprise me. I don't have any ideas who it might be, but I am on the road a lot. Uncle, you know better than most, treachery is the way of the world."

Alexander nodded. Good answer. Good boy.

"Do you miss your father, Nicky?"

That took Nicky aback.

"Sure, I miss him. He had his troubles but he was okay. He probably never quite accepted me, but he loved me. I have no complaints."

"How would my son answer that same question?"

Nicky laughed. "Probably not too different. Different reasons and circumstances. But he knows you love him—and Helena."

Nicky crossed himself in the Orthodox manner of touching his right shoulder first. Alexander had never seen him do that before.

"I think his mother's medical condition keeps him away too."

Nicky's phone chirped and he hit the receive button without answering. He listened for a couple minutes and finally asked a question: "You got a name?" After a few seconds he gave a command, "Find out everything you can on this man Burke."

He looked at his Uncle and said: "Pauline's phone was programmed to call a couple of numbers, including a bakery in Belgium in her phone. La Bon Bouche. The place doesn't exist but our men found the man at the end of the line. The man, of course, claimed innocence and said he knew nothing, but after talking things over, he remembered he was working for a man."

"Burke."

"Yes. Burke."

Nicky held up the phone to show a picture of the mutilated body of Burke's man in Brussels.

"There's also a number that goes directly to an off-the-grid bulletin board Burke uses. I think Mr. Burke should get a look at his man," Nicky said, smiling as he sent a text to the man who had provided him the update. "We have the interrogation on video. This Mr. Burke will enjoy that even more."

"I was told the man who had been hired to enter our gates was Colonel Grayson," Alexander spoke.

"They might be working together," Nicky responded, looking up.

"Give Mr. Burke and Colonel Grayson your full attention, Nicky."

"I'm on it," he replied, leaving the last third of his cigar in the Waterford crystal bowl. "By the way, Uncle, either Grayson or Burke have men who have been watching the Gulfstream and who have been watching us here. We've picked them up for questioning."

"You have done well, Nicky. I believe your father would be proud, even if he had another road planned out for you."

Nicky nodded in appreciation.

"Before you go, there is one more thing, Nicky."

"Yes Uncle?"

"Even without Pauline on the loose, the days are about to become infinitely more dangerous. I need you safe. I need you sharp. We'll head back to Geneva in the morning. I want you to spend some time each evening with Sophia and the kids. No late nights in the bars on your way home from the office. Focus yourself. I think it best that you not visit Patmos for a period of time. Others need to stay focused on their work as well."

Nicky felt like a lemon was blocking his airwaves as he responded, "I understand Uncle."

32

New York City

THINGS WERE UNRAVELING FAST for Burke. First, Pauline. Then Henri, his operative in Brussels, didn't answer the phone when Burke called him for a status update. Burke tried numerous times over the course of several hours. Then someone picked up. A woman asked who was calling and how she might be of help. In his years of working with Henri, no one else had ever picked up that line. Burke'd give ten to one odds it was a police woman.

Henri was blown. That told Burke there was no longer a question Pauline had been captured, interrogated, and had the bakery connection twisted out of her. No doubt, painfully.

Who got to Henri? Alexander's forces or the police working on behalf of Alexander or the police working independently? If the it was Alexander's soldiers, Henri was not in a good place.

Something else was wrong and it was staring Burke in the face. When he left the street level door of the Oak Room, eschewing the path through the ornate lobby of the Plaza, he followed his standard operating procedure when on a dangerous assignment. Walk fast. Walk slow. Stop. Turn around and retrace steps. Use the reflections in windows to see if he was being followed. Grab a cab. Exit the cab two blocks later and grab another going the opposite direction. Be unpredictable. He followed the same arduous procedure exiting the Peninsula. He again saw nothing. He was alone. Invisible.

But somehow he knew he wasn't.

He paid the driver to drop him off three blocks from his seedy motel. But half a block before arriving at the blinking neon entrance he realized he had seen the bum who appeared to be sleeping in a doorway before. Burke had a remarkable memory for faces. Where had he seen him? It had to be in Hell's Kitchen. Was it? He snapped his fingers. He had it. The bum was in a business suit drinking a cup of coffee in the diner across from his previous motel.

Or maybe not. But I think yes. Yes. Same man.

Burke, thirty-seven years old, a veteran of Iraq and Afghanistan—always "outside the wire" on the most dangerous assignments—had stayed alive by trusting his instincts.

In his first years of lethal assignments he had always prayed before he entered the arena of battle. When had he stopped? And why? Was it the amount of blood on his hands? He grew up as a Sunday School and church kid. He knew his Bible from start to finish. He had always loved the stories of David. Shepherd boy. Giant killer. Writer of the most beautiful words of worship ever written. King. But the man and his stories had come to mean something different to him when he became a warrior himself. Under an azure Afghan sky Burke had fully realized that David was more than a shepherd and songwriter. That was only half the picture. He was much more than the sanitized version he had been taught as a kid. David, the man after God's heart, was a brutal mercenary; a warrior's warrior; a stone cold killer. He was a man whose hands were covered with the blood of both the guilty and innocent. Not just his hands. He could bathe in the blood he shed. That took a toll on you, no matter how close to God you thought you were.

As a boy David sang songs to soothe the spirit of a mad king. Burke suspected that David sang songs as an old man to soothe his own troubled memories.

As a Special Forces soldier, Burke had followed the same bloody path. But that didn't adequately explain why he no longer prayed. That happened in Operation Desert Scorpion on June 25, 2003.

Burke pictured the man in the suit and compared him to the bum in the doorway again. It was a match. Houston, we have a problem. Burke knew there was a time to attack and that there were times when it was best not to let an adversary know he had been spotted. Burke never broke stride as he entered the lobby without a care in the world and hit the call button for the elevator, never looking back. He walked quietly down the threadbare-carpeted hallway. He had already been spotted so if someone was waiting for him, he already knew Burke was coming. The bum would have called ahead. He would be on high alert. There would be no surprise.

He turned the key in his room slowly and carefully. He knew instantly it was empty.

Time to find the tracking bug. No question, there was a tracer. Over the next two hours his hands and eyes worked every square centimeter of every item he carried with him, from briefcase to shoes to toothpaste tube to every stitch of clothing. He wasn't gentle. It would all be thrown away anyway. He opened his iPad and studied the hardware with a magnifying glass he retracted from a Swiss Army knife. Just when he was ready to give up his eye caught a nearly imperceptible flaw in the stitching on one of the cloth handles of his duffle bag.

He slit it carefully and found the tiny GPS transmitter, no larger than a small matchstick. Burke cursed. How long had it been secured there? From that moment on, he had never been alone. Not for the entire operation to capture the scratches and scrawls inside Alexander's journal. Even as he wondered what his next step would be to stay alive and make someone pay for this incursion past every safeguard he thought he had constructed, he took inventory of his decisions and movements. Where had he got careless? Someone had planted a homing device on him without him having a clue. Other than Pauline, he couldn't think of anyone else with access or any egregious errors on his part. That meant whoever was tracking him was good—probably the man who hired him who spoke through a metallic modulator. Burke looked at the small cylindrical stick that was no more than half an inch long. They had put eyes on him, like the bum, but hadn't attempted to follow him on his street movements where they would be vulnerable to being detected by his counter surveillance. They didn't have to. They always knew where his home base was.

Burke suspected the flurry of phone calls from his client had nothing to do with triangulating his exact location at any given moment. It was a ruse to make him think that was what he was trying to do. That way he would be less suspicious of other tracking methods, which they already had in place to pinpoint his whereabouts. The red herring had worked.

His mind went to the face of the one man he knew who could pull this off. He wasn't the only man who could do it, but probably the only one he knew personally. His former commanding officer, Colonel Arnold "Arnie" Grayson, an immoral, amoral sociopath. Burke caught him with his hand in the proverbial cookie jar, elbow deep—selling sophisticated weaponry and tactical gear to the enemy. He was sure that was only the tip of the iceberg. Had he not been forced to flee and disappear after Grayson set him up to be ambushed, he was sure that Grayson was screwing the US Army in a variety of ways. After all, he was the man responsible to distribute money to informants in the Iraqi theater of operations.

Burke stole a jeep in Tikrit and drove like a madman to the hill city of Aqrah. His escape over the border into the town of Batman, Turkey, included shooting his way out of an abandoned village on the Iraqi side of the border. He hit pay dirt in that unnamed village. While hiding under floorboards to recuperate, he found a cache of 30 one-kilo gold bars. He claimed squatters' rights on the gold and when he saw a patrol jeep racing into the town, he fled, guns blazing, with more than sixty-six pounds of bullion that afforded him the financial means to hire a boat in Hatay, Turkey, and then sail to Crete and then into the dangerous port of Naples, Italy. He took the train to Zurich, still in possession of twenty-five gold bars. The price of gold at the end of 2003 had edged up to $400 an ounce. He delivered his spoils of war to a discrete private bank on the Bahnhofstrasse. It became the initial $350 thousand investment for a paramilitary startup. He bought a new name and did all in his power to embrace a new outlook on life: cynicism and unmitigated self-interest.

Burke was his middle name and that is the only thing he kept from his past. Maybe keeping his middle name had been his singular hold on where he came from and the man he once was.

Through a simple online search, he learned he was listed as MIA and presumed dead. He had been awarded a Purple Heart and a Medal of Valor posthumously. He would thank Grayson for doing something that would make his parents proud, but he knew anything Grayson did was for himself and himself alone. Dead. Burke decided it was better that way. But he was sad that meant not telling his parents he was still alive. Maybe better for them to think he was dead. They wouldn't like the man he had become.

Any chance of rediscovering his lost faith was destroyed when he made a dangerous trip back to Baghdad. From two-hundred yards away, Burke spun a 2.75-inch-long sniper bullet from an M24—the US Army's adaptation of the Remington 700—through the left eye of Lieutenant Colonel Dan Samblin, the man in charge of the MPs in Iraq, who ratted him out to Grayson. Grayson was already stateside or he would have died the same night.

Why had he let Grayson live? That was the man who had ruined his life. Maybe he was afraid to find out what else the man had done to those whom he loved after he disappeared off the grid of the living.

Fifteen years had passed. He had built a very specialized and successful business that was fifty percent payment up front and fifty percent upon completion of assignment. The margins were enormous.

Maybe this had nothing to do with Grayson but for some reason it had his scent wafting over it. He wondered for the millionth time why he had let the man live.

So what now? Drop the GPS transmitter in the pocket of someone catching a flight in the opposite direction as he was heading as a diversion? Destroy it and make a run for it? Or use it as bait?

The answer was obvious.

The homeless man was still sleeping in the same doorway. Burke had the cab stop so he could jump out. He dropped a $10 bill in the man's begging cap and said, "God bless you." The man never responded. He was good and stayed in character, the only reason he was still alive.

He hopped back in the backseat of the cab and told the driver, "JFK. British Airways terminal. Last flight leaves in ninety minutes. There's an extra fifty for you if you can get there in less than thirty."

He reached in the side pocket of his Harris Tweed jacket that he used to dress up his jeans for international travel. He looked at the GPS from every angle. He needed a new supplier. He didn't have anything this powerful and small.

Let's see if this reels in whoever wants to know where you are before your flight leaves.

His flight to Paris—he wouldn't be taking British Airways to Heathrow in London—would give him a chance to plan how to start working up the food chain to discover—or if it was Grayson, confirm—who had hired him. The only question was if no one made a move at him in the airport. Hold it and let them know where he was—or slough it off on someone and confirm he had discovered it.

He looked at his phone. No text messages. No word from his watcher outside Alexander's townhome or the man who just arrived in Fayetteville, Arkansas, to see if he could discover what happened to Pauline. There wouldn't be anything from the latter. He knew Jules had killed her or secreted her to a spot where he would never discover her in time.

He tapped a game app icon with a smiling frog to check his electronic bulletin board. A message had been posted to a new thread with two files. He tapped the first image file.

Henri—or what was left of Henri—stared back at him through empty eye sockets. Someone had surgically opened his lower stomach, which was an empty crater. His naked body was a mosaic of burns and slices. His genitals were missing.

Burke slowed his breathing, even as the cab raced through traffic.

The next file was a video. Burke didn't want to open it, but Henri had been a loyal employee and friend for many years. The picture image of the short movie was crystal clear. Henri was very much alive. Henri was being forced to stay on his feet as he staggered around a wooden post. One end of his small intestine had been nailed to the post. Every time Henri started to fall, one or two men would catch him and keep him on two feet. They would then push him forward as seven meters of small intestine was pulled from his body and wound around the post. Each meter, the men screamed the same questions in his eyeless face.

"Where is his base of operations? How do you connect with him? How do we find Burke?"

Pauline and Henri both dead. Time to pull everyone off the operation and tell them to disappear. He didn't care that it was doubtful he would ever see the second half of the blood money on the Alexander contract.

A reflex inside him wanted to go back a few years and say a prayer for Pauline and Henri and maybe himself. He knew the Sunday School answer was that no matter what you've done bad in life, you can always start over with a clean slate. He shrugged the thought away. There is too much blood on my hands. Soon there will be more.

33

The Ozark National Forest

PAULINE OPENED HER EYES, STILL groggy from her ordeal the day before. At least she assumed it was the day before.

I'm alive. Spared again. But for what?

She sat up slowly. There was no curtain on the window and dancing shafts of starlight filtered into her room, turning blackness to smudges of charcoal gray and azure blue accents.

She stood up and the rough wooden floorboards creaked and groaned loudly. She tiptoed to the window. She was upstairs in a cabin surrounded by a dense forest. She moved to the front window. A small yard, no more than fifty meters deep was swallowed into the woods at its abrupt end. To the left was a small structure. He first thought was storage, but the rough hewn side wall didn't reach floor or ceiling. A small barn?

Her bed was a double with a soft down mattress. A single dresser had a line of plush dolls arranged on it. She looked at the bedspread. It was actually a quilt with a mosaic of flowers. The nightstand had a small lamp shaped like a kitten on it. The only other piece of furniture was a small writing desk. A row of ceramic cats looked at her. In front of them was a glass of water and a small plate with cut fruit, cheese, and crackers, covered by the sheen of Saran wrap. Her stomach growled on cue. Her mouth was dry.

She crept over, planning to eat and drink slowly. The plate and glass were empty in less than a minute.

Now I'll have to go to the bathroom.

She looked at the door with fear. What lay beyond it? Jules and other Alexander men? Could she even open it? It might be locked. She was probably a prisoner. She looked out the window again. There was a shallow roof that covered a wrap around porch. She could climb on that and jump from there—maybe a twelve-foot drop—without major injury. But where would she go?

She looked at the ceramic cats thoughtfully. If she broke off the head of one she would have a dangerous weapon to stab or slash with. She would love to drive a spiked shard of ceramic into Jules' eye socket. When had she ever thought things like that? Living in fear for six months, being shot, and running for your life could do that to you.

She felt her shoulder and realized someone had taken off her clothes and dressed the wound. She was wearing an oversized pair of men's pajamas. How long had she been asleep? Her eyes were already wanting to close. Apparently not long enough.

She mustered her courage and treaded toward the door. She opened it and it creaked loud enough to wake someone in a neighboring state. It didn't matter. She was where she was. She couldn't kill Jules with a broken cat—and probably not with an Uzi.

She peered down a short narrow hallway. There was a door at the other end. Undoubtedly another bedroom. Halfway down the hall was a night light. It was placed in a socket outside an open door. Had to be a bathroom.

The carpet runner muffled her footsteps a little, but occasionally she would step on wood strip that was just waiting to holler. She turned into the bathroom, shut the door, and turned on the light. It was a tiny room with a small shower, a toilet, a recessed bookcase with toiletries and supplies, and a small sink. On it was a towel, a bar of soap, a small glass with a new toothbrush in it, and toothpaste. The bare necessities. All she needed.

She used the toilet, considered a shower, but settled for a quick sponge bath with the washcloth. She brushed her teeth. Took a look in the mirror at her dark ringed sunken eyes. She examined her shoulder closely. The wound was covered with a thick unguent poultice and held in place with a gauze wrap. Amazingly the pain was manageable. A home remedy? She wanted to lift the poultice to see the state of the bullet wound, but figured it was better off left alone at the moment.

She knew she had to figure out where she was and plan what to do next. But that would have to wait. She was warm with food and water inside her. She wasn't exactly clean or pain free, but her conditions were reasonable to great under the circumstances. She was too tired to think anyway. She went back to the little girl bedroom, shut the door, pulled the blankets up tight under her chin, and was asleep in less than thirty seconds.

34

Bentonville, Arkansas

REVEREND DWIGHT GARRISON WOKE WITH a start. He sat up wide-eyed. He had soaked the bed in sweat a second night in a row. His wife Judy mumbled something to him but wasn't quite awake and rolled away from him, never opening her eyes.

Good. This was his problem. He didn't want to bother her rest. He didn't want her to see him like this.

What was going on? Why was he dreaming so vividly of war, plague, and pestilence? Where had such vivid images of tortured death come from? He didn't watch violent movies or play violent games. He was taught as a child to guard his heart and mind from images of evil and that was how he had conducted his life.

He walked into the small kitchen of the three-bedroom ranch house on the corner of the church property. He took a glass from the cupboard and filled it with water. He smoothed back his bedraggled hair. Wow. What a dream—what a nightmare. It was a vision of hell on earth. In the middle of the carnage was Jonathan Alexander, riding a huge red horse.

Their last meeting was both remarkable and unremarkable.

What was most remarkable was that one of the richest men in the world had visited him three days ago. Him. Dwight Garrison. Pastor of the Mount Olive Independent Baptist Church. And not for the first time.

He sat down at the kitchen table to clear his mind and say a quick prayer. His Bible was next to him, still open to Revelation 9.

He half stood to return to the bedroom but realized he wasn't going to fall back asleep anytime soon … not after seeing the blood seeping from the eyes, the nostrils, the ears, and every other orifice of the children. Not after seeing blackened fields littered with men, women, and children in the last stages of starvation, stomachs bloated, eyes vacant. Their mouths opened and closed to voice the moans of their misery, but no sound coming out. No, he would not fall back asleep easily after seeing missiles turn airplanes into fiery infernos. In those scenes he could hear the screaming of the victims.

His meeting with Alexander was also remarkable for the specific line of questioning. The international businessman always wanted to know more about the Book of Revelation in broad terms. But this visit had been different. The man had something specific on his mind.

"I'm just a country preacher, Mr. Alexander, why do you come to see me?" he had asked.

"Maybe God brought me to you."

"But you've told me you're not sure you believe in God."

"Consider me a seeker of truth," Alexander had answered.

In previous conversations, Alexander would ask an occasional question and listen. Garrison would do most of the speaking.

Not yesterday. After his dreams, the meeting felt like it had taken place a week ago.

He had never seen the man so animated as he asked his questions. What armies will be at Armageddon? Are you sure? Tell me again what factors will start the final battle? Who is the Antichrist? Who is the Beast? How will they be recognized? Who is the Whore of Babylon? What form will Christ take? Will the Beast know his role in waging war against Christ? Will he know the prophecies of John? Will he think he can win? What is the timetable?

This didn't seem theoretical to the man. It was as if Alexander had been visited by the supernatural and knew something was coming.

When Garrison felt the call to be a preacher and attended Bible College in Chesterton, Indiana, he had yearned for deep conversations like this. Well, not like this, but intense dialog on Scripture and spiritual matters. He pictured being a pastor as preaching twice on Sunday, leading a Bible study and prayer meeting on Wednesday night, and a series of hour-long meetings Monday through Saturday with sincere seekers who wanted to know how God's Word applied to this or that situation in their life.

Those Monday-through-Saturday, heart-to-heart encounters had been few and far between, replaced by meetings to make sure there was enough money to keep the lights turned on, buy supplies, and ensure he had a salary. In the seven or eight times he and Alexander met, he kept looking for signs that he was boring the man. But Alexander never looked at his watch or phone. He gave Garrison his undivided attention. He seemed to cling to every word. He wrote nothing but Garrison wondered if he was recording the conversation because he kept looking at a small jeweled pin on his lapel.

I probably got carried away with such a receptive audience and waxed a little too eloquent at times, Garrison thought, finally mustering a small smile. A dying child, being torn apart by vultures, reappeared from his dream. The smile was gone.

But for this last conversation the billionaire directed the dialog with his questions, including a few that threw Garrison for a loop. They felt … strange. Eerie. They were troubling. Especially in the last moments of their time together. No wonder his dreams were so surreal. Was that the only thing he needed to understand to explain his dreams?

Alexander had repositioned himself in the chair across from Garrison, looked at him with dark hazel eyes, and said, "I just need to clarify something we discussed earlier. What is your understanding of confidentiality between a minister and someone he is counseling?"

After a brief pause Garrison answered, "If someone comes to me with a personal spiritual issue, then I can't legally or morally reveal the contents of our meeting."

"I want to remind you that I've come to you with a personal spiritual issue," Alexander had said quickly, too quickly. "Will you honor this meeting with a continued commitment to confidentiality?"

"I've already answered this question in previous meetings Mr. Alexander."

"Call me Doubting Thomas. I need to hear the words again. Will you keep our conversation confidential? No matter what?"

"Yes sir, I will."

"I've been given promises before that were broken, seemingly on a whim. How do I know you are different?"

"If you care to talk to anyone in my congregation or family, I think they will tell you I am a man of my word," Garrison answered.

"That isn't practical and it won't be necessary," Alexander said. "I think I trust you."

He had never had anyone be so direct on the issue of confidentiality. Despite a twinge of concern, he assumed—or was it that he *hoped*—at the moment that it had to do with Jonathan Alexander's legendary aversion to publicity. If the meeting had ended like he hoped it would, Garrison would tell Alexander that if he accepted Jesus Christ as his Lord and Savior, he would need to make a public confession of his faith and be baptized. But that opportunity never arrived.

There had been a rare pause in their conversation. Garrison had run out of words. Alexander remained silent for a moment. His eyes seem to bore into Garrison's soul. It felt strange. He wanted to believe the man was pondering the offer of eternal life Garrison had just presented to him. But Alexander's next questions, his final questions, were again about the Beast.

"Reverend Garrison, in your considerable knowledge of what you call the End Times, do you believe that a man can consciously volunteer to assist God in bringing all this about? Can a man choose to assume a role in creating the conditions for Armageddon? As one example, could a man choose to be the Beast?"

Unlike their previous encounters, Garrison didn't know how to answer immediately. What was the man asking? What was he getting at? Did he know something? Had he recognized evil in someone?

After another moment of silence Garrison said, "There are Christians who have committed their lives to seeing the Gospel preached to the ends of the earth in order to meet that condition for Christ's Second Coming. I don't know of anyone working toward Armageddon—something no one wants to see happen—but I can see why you asked it that way. The two events are connected. Do you know someone who wants to be the Beast?"

He smiled but Alexander just stared back.

"There are those who have been committed to establishing and preserving a Jewish nation for that same reason," Reverend Garrison awkwardly continued. "God will use whom He will, but yes, I have to assume that a man can consciously volunteer to be part of God's glorious plan for the End Times."

He planned to clarify that he didn't think a role as specific as the Beast would be within human purview. But Alexander cut him off and stood abruptly.

He had hoped beyond hope to once again ask Alexander if he was ready to accept Jesus as his Lord and Savior, but the man was done talking. He had extended his hand, and the two men shook hands.

"Thank you, Reverend Garrison. That is exactly what I wanted to hear. You have been most helpful."

Garrison wanted to say something more but couldn't muster his thoughts to get even a word out.

Alexander paused before he reached the office door, pulled a notecard out of his jacket pocket, and placed it carefully on the corner of Garrison's desk, and looked him in the eyes.

"I know you have not accepted my previous offers of financial remuneration. I thank you for your generous gift of time. But please reconsider using this humble expression of my gratitude in whatever way you believe it will best assist you in your ministry. The user name is the same, the password has been updated. It will expire at week's end and the money will no longer be available for you to use."

Then the man was gone.

Garrison had watched from his small office window as the black Range Rover pulled out of the gravel parking lot.

He held the quality card stock in his hand and looked at the four lines. The user name, the password, the most recent deposit, and the balance. The latest deposit was $5 million, bringing the total to $11 million plus interest.

What would he do with that kind of money? What had he said that Alexander wanted to hear so badly and reward so generously?

He got up from the kitchen table and looked outside at a brilliant night sky shimmering with stars and a full moon. It was as large as any harvest moon he had ever seen. But instead of a yellow-gold hue, it almost had a red tint to it. He shuddered. Was this a full blood moon he had read about?

He turned and looked at his open Bible. He flipped forward three pages. Revelation 13:1 in the good old King James Version read:

"And I stood upon the sand of the sea, and saw a beast rise up out of the sea, having seven heads and ten horns, and upon his horns ten crowns, and upon his heads the name of blasphemy."

Garrison stood up and refilled his empty water glass.

Was the explanation of Alexander's interest in him—in his questions during their time together—as obvious as it seemed in retrospect? Had Garrison been fueling the imagination of a madman intent on mass murder? Was Alexander using him to inspire genocide? Was Alexander volunteering to be the Beast?

He didn't want to acknowledge that possibility. But it was there. Staring him right in the face.

Can a man choose to assume a role in creating the conditions for Armageddon?

He was suddenly sick to his stomach. Should he go to authorities? Who would he call? The FBI? But what would he tell them? I think I've been giving spiritual guidance to a man who wants to be the Beast of Revelation?

Even if he could get someone to listen, what of his promise of confidentiality? It wasn't a vague promise with conditions on it—Alexander made sure of that. But what if the man was considering what he saw in his dreams?

Should he confront Alexander directly? But how? Their last meeting had the feeling of a definite finality to it. He suspected—no, he knew—Alexander would not be reaching out to him again. He didn't have a phone number to call him anyway. All incoming calls had been blocked. But did it really matter? If Alexander's thinking was as diabolically crazy as he thought it might be, would the man listen to reason? Not likely.

But was that the point? He couldn't do … nothing. If he was bound by a solemn oath to not divulge the contents of their conversation, he had to get to Alexander directly. He knew the man kept homes all over the world, but his primary residence was outside of Geneva, Switzerland. *Do I just knock on his front door?*

He still had a passport from a biblical tour of the Holy Land a few years back. But no way could he afford a trip to Europe.

He opened the back of his Bible and picked up the thick card with four rows of numbers on it.

I can't just do nothing.

35

New York City

THE MADISON CLUB, JUST EAST of Central Park, between Park
and Madison Avenues on 68th Street, has no signage to announce its
presence. The dinner club and its small membership list rest in the
shadows. If you belong in it, you know it exists and know where it's
located. If you don't belong there—and that would be all but three
hundred members and their guests—you probably have never heard
of it.

Unless a member accompanies you or sponsors you for a dinner
meeting in one of the small private alcoves surrounding the main
restaurant floor, you can't get in even if you know its location.

Though only two of the men spoke, three men dined together. You
don't order off a menu at the Madison Club. Whatever the Le Cordon
Bleu master chef prepared is what you eat. And you never complain. It
took them almost three hours to work through a fourteen course French
dinner. The hors d'oeuvre was saumon fume. The bouillabaisse, the
potage for the evening, was divine. Gnocchi served as the farineux. Sole
in a white wine, garlic, and butter sauce was the poisson. The entrée was
canard medallions, sautéed with ground cherries, caramelized onions,
and white port. The lemon sorbet cleared the palate for the relevé, a
rare boeuf filet with peppercorns and béarnaise sauce.

Jack Marcum, the third man at the table, the one who never spoke, was dining at the Madison Club for the first time and thought the meal was overkill. He had assumed the sorbet was dessert, not a respite to prepare for another meat dish. He marveled at the fat man's appetite. The thin man held his own, too, but always left something on the plate. How many names for a main dish could there be? And when he saw the waiters approaching with another round of fresh plates, he wondered why they couldn't combine a few courses.

The legumes course consisted of cauliflower mornay with a small side of roasted tomatoes. Marcum assumed there would be actual legumes but wasn't about to question anything. A salade vert followed. The fat man, his boss, was relentless. He cleaned his plates on yet two more courses.

The savoreaux was a pungent welsh rarebit. Marcum was long done being hungry. But he nibbled politely, even if the rarebit was not to his liking. Duty called. The cheese board with Rocquefort Societe and Pont-l'Eveque was where Jack drew the line. One whiff of the latter and he had to stifle a gag.

How can people eat something that smells like something my bulldog leaves on the sidewalk?

Dessert began with strawberries and grapes, but that was only phase one. Chocolate gateaux wasn't far behind.

Marcum swallowed as little as he could. His jaw began to hurt from pretending to chew more than he ingested.

Marcum lost count of how many styles of wine were served. He took a sip of each but the sommelier never took the hint and always poured him a full measure. Marcum guessed the wine he had *not* drunk tonight cost more than all the Budweiser he had downed in the previous year.

He followed the two men up a sweeping staircase to the Churchill Lounge where he joined them in lighting up a rare pre-embargo Montecristo No. 2—one of Castro's favorite smokes. He took one sip of the Marquis de Montesquious 1904 Vintage brandy.

The fat man was not happy that the Rémy Martin Louis XIII Black Pearl Limited Edition cognac was not available.

"A bottle costs more than $20 thousand," Heller whispered to him when Wannegrin went to use the restroom.

That definitely cost more than all the beer Marcum had drunk in his life, and as college freshman, he had consumed his share of Bud and Miller.

It was now after midnight. The conversation appeared to have run its course. The two speakers watched each other across a haze of smoke, Marcum between them but invisible, just like his boss wanted it, his back to the wall. Marcum was relaxed but watched everything. That was his job.

He couldn't follow the full details of their discussion. The men spoke cryptically. He knew they couldn't decide what to do with "the little" they got. His boss wasn't officially authorized to mount covert operations. Marcum also knew that Emanuel Heller did whatever he wanted to do.

"So much effort with so little to show for it. Now what? That is the question, my friend," said Undersecretary of State Emanuel Heller.

"You already know what I think we do with it," Wannegrin said through clenched teeth.

The morbidly obese Heller pondered Wannegrin's response as he blew a smoke ring from his third cigar of the evening. Marcum watched it spiral lazily toward the copper-plated ceiling. Heller was seventy-two years old, but he liked to liven conversation with the declaration that his doctor said he had the body of an eighty-two-year-old man.

In a meeting the previous week, Marcum heard Heller brag to the surgeon general: "I am one-hundred-and-sixty-pounds overweight, have high blood pressure, and bad kidneys—and I plan to do nothing about it. Life's too short to not savor its finest."

Marcum could have added that Heller had pasty white skin save for a few red blotchy rashes. But in Heller's role of man behind the throne, none of that mattered. He possessed a near eidetic memory, with a brain filled to overflowing with history, political intrigue, and the secrets of everyone who mattered in Washington, D.C., and maybe every other country.

Marcum watched, fascinated.

Heller looked at the man across from him. Marcum had experienced that stare first-hand. It felt like the small narrow jet black eyes were probing you, looking for access to your inner workings— and succeeding. Heller was trying to do the same thing to Walter Wannegrin. Marcum wondered if Wannegrin, a formidable man in his own right, got the same sense of being opened up on an operating table as mere mortals? What was Wannegrin thinking? Marcum was certain Wannegrin was doing all he could to contain his anger. He was being grilled and chastised by a man he called Manny and who called him Wally. They might be old friends but Heller knew how to twist the knife while smiling, consuming mass quantities of food, and looking for all the world as if nothing was bothering him.

Wannegrin and Heller were roughly the same age, but Heller looked ten years older. Maybe twenty. Heller had commented on that before the first course arrived, saying, "Wally do you look like a young man next to me because you look so good or I look so bad?"

Marcum watched, for the first time feeling uncomfortable in the two men's presence, as Heller continued to gaze at Wannegrin closely.

"Is there any truth to the rumor Alexander has had a stroke?" Heller probed, breaking the silent struggle of wills.

"We would never know if he did," Wannegrin answered. "He looks fine in public appearances."

Marcum had been with the two men at dinners such as this. The conversation was not flowing like usual. There was a palpable tension in the air.

"Who is Alexander working with, Walter?"

"Alexander isn't a team player, Manny, and you know it. He's not part of a machine because in his mind he is the machine. He works with no one because he trusts no one. That's what made this incursion into his inner circle so tough."

"Wally, I must look for someone else to reach Alexander. I credit you with nearly pulling off the impossible. For that I am thankful. But we don't have enough to do anything but discredit the man as delusional. There's a lot of ways he can spin that. We just didn't get enough. We need to wrap this chapter up and put a bow on it. There will be another day."

"Manny, my friend, we can blow him out of the water with what we have. Whatever whacky plan he has cooked up, we can stop it before it starts. 'I will ride the blood red horse of the Apocalypse.' C'mon, Manny. He's up to something big and something evil. He's so full of himself he might want to best Hitler and Stalin for genocide."

"I agree with what you are saying. But Wally, we're still nearly blind. We don't know who else is involved in whatever Alexander is working on. I know you don't agree with me, but it is possible he might be one cog in a machine. Moving on him could free others to avoid scrutiny."

"He's not a cog and you know it, Manny."

"But who knows Wally? He might have been writing allegorically about a new business venture, not literally about wreaking destruction on the earth's population. Wally, I think we sit on this for the time being."

Wannegrin reddened. Heller knew it was time to back off.

"Excuse me Wally, I must use the little boy's room"

He pushed down on the arm rests and managed to shift more than four hundred pounds to a standing position.

WANNEGRIN FUMED WHILE HELLER WAS away from their nook in the cigar lounge.

It was true. He had failed. It didn't matter that Grayson and whomever he subcontracted the job to had been the ones directly responsible for a botched operation. Ultimately, it was on him. He had let down his old friend Emanuel Heller, and along with him both of the countries he loved so much. Flushing 25 million dollars down the drain chafed at him.

We must wrap this chapter up.

Wannegrin knew what Heller was asking for and he would never make the man, no matter how much he infuriated him, ask for it directly. That's not how they did things. Stopping the conversation right there was probably Heller's way of keeping Marcum out of the loop.

Wannegrin didn't need any prodding from Heller on what to do next. Grayson was a loose cannon and absolutely untrustworthy. Walter had already ordered a team from Blackwater to terminate the contract and tie up all loose ends. Permanently. He didn't like that such actions were sometimes necessary. He was a man of peace. He was one of the few who believed fervently it was possible to have a Palestinian nation sit alongside the nation of Israeli. But though regrettable, the ends really did sometimes justify the means. David didn't face Goliath to talk over their differences.

"Wally, dinner was sublime," Heller said as he eased his weight back in the chair across from him. "You must let me pick up the tab."

"Manny, you probably forgot, but there is nothing so Philistine as the exchange of money to ruin a perfectly splendid meal. The cost was so little that perhaps they will forget about it. If not, they will send me a bill."

"Are you sure, Wally? I don't think they'll forget about the cognac."

"Manny, I insist."

"You must let me treat you next time, Wally. Really, you must."

"Absolutely. You can be sure that the tab for dinner is yours next time."

JACK MARCUM KEPT HIS FACE impassive but smiled quickly on the inside. He had worked as an administrative assistant for Emanuel Heller for three years, and in his own personal experience, he had never once seen the man pay for a meal. Heck, if they went to Starbucks, Jack had to pay. Emanuel Heller would fumble for his wallet only to discover he had left it in the car. Whether they were dining with a senator or lobbyist or captain of industry, the same ritual of offering to buy the next meal was replayed.

He looked at the two men circumspectly. How do you read what just transpired? Neither was happy with the other, but neither was willing to pursue the track of disagreement any further. They looked at each other with an appraisal Marcum had never seen. So what would he report?

Marcum could type more than one hundred words a minute. He was also a Navy Seal who knew at least one hundred ways to kill or disable an adversary. That made him invaluable to Heller.

What Heller didn't know was that less than twelve hours ago, Marcum had accepted a new assignment. He wouldn't be resigning from Heller's office, however. The president's chief of staff, Gwen Hampton, made it clear when laying out what was needed that working for Heller was a requisite of concurrently working directly for the POTUS.

Marcum admired Heller. He would never do anything to injure his boss. But Hampton was right. Heller's health was deteriorating rapidly and the legend was holding secrets that would go to the grave with him, maybe sooner than later.

Marcum felt a twinge of discomfort and guilt that Hampton let him know he would be receiving a generous stipend for his service to the President, paid through back channels into an offshore account.

He wasn't against personal profit but it put a taint on what he would do for free out of red, white, and blue patriotism.

THE MARINE HELICOPTER SET DOWN at the East 34th Street Heliport. It took two men inside the craft, one on each arm, pulling and Marcum pushing from below to get Emanuel Heller aboard.

Heller and Marcum strapped in and the craft immediately lifted off for the 90-minute hop to Washington, D.C.

Heller looked out the window to catch a quick glance at One World Trade Center, better known as the Freedom Tower, the signature landmark on the south end of Manhattan. If anyone had listened to Heller, the beacon would never have been erected. Why build a 1,776-foot target to taunt enemies who need no taunting?

The pilot banked to the south east and the East River and Williamsport section of Brooklyn slipped below.

Emanuel sat back and sighed. His first move against Alexander was not a total disaster, but close enough to go in the loss column. Heller had already pieced together enough seemingly random events to suspect that the megalomaniacal billionaire was up to some evil deeds. The pages captured from Alexander's journal confirmed those suspicions, but did not provide the detail to prove—or avert—anything.

"Did you enjoy dinner?" he shouted to Marcum above the roar of the rotors.

"It was amazing, boss," Marcum hollered back.

"Then why didn't you eat the cheese?"

"I've never had a chance to acquire the taste," Marcum responded, shocked that Heller noticed anything he ate or didn't eat at the Madison Club.

"We'll work on that," Heller yelled.

Heller smiled, knowing the distress this would cause his aide-de-camp.

Emanuel thought of his lifelong friend. Wannegrin was ostensibly retired from the necessity of work, having built several international companies that were being run with spectacular success by his sons. He split his year between a condo in the One57 Tower, a five-hundred-acre equestrian estate in Fairfax County, Virginia, and a mansion built inside a fortified wall of stone and iron atop the rocks overlooking the Sea of Galilee in Tiberius, Israel.

Wannegrin was a friend of politicians and movers and shakers in both countries. Heller never asked him which country held his highest allegiance. He didn't have to. Heller knew Wally was a Mossad sayanim—volunteer helper. Wally undoubtedly shared state secrets he picked up about one country with the other, but Heller trusted that Wannegrin fundamentally had the best interests of both Israel and the US in his heart, so he sometimes threw Walter a juicy morsel to barter with. Yes, Wannegrin had a good heart, but it didn't mean he was averse to making an extra million or two with forbidden knowledge he acquired from his friend.

For the first time in his relationship with Walter Wannegrin, however, Emanuel Heller wondered if he could trust his friend. Something was wrong.

Heller remembered a *Wall Street Journal* article outlining a deal the two titans had explored together more than twenty-five years ago. Was that the ground zero of Wannegrin's hatred of Alexander? He would look up the details. It was smart to keep tabs on both enemies and friends.

I know you, Wally. Something's up. You're not being totally honest with me. Why didn't you deliver the goods? Why does it feel like Alexander didn't get your best shot?

With no companies to lead had Wannegrin lost his edge? Was it age? When had he ever seen the Israeli accept failure with such emotional detachment? What wasn't Walter sharing? Did Alexander have something he was holding over Walter's head? Did he have a way of damaging Wannegrin's fortune? If there was one weakness in his lifelong friend, it was avarice.

Heller knew that greed was one of the most vulnerable, unprotected, and self-blinding sides a man could offer the world—especially his enemies. Had Alexander found a foothold?

Heller decided as a young man that public service, not personal gain, would drive his life. His family was well off but nothing close to the wealth that often surrounded him most of seventy-two years. He had lived contentedly and comfortably in the same brownstone townhouse in Georgetown that his parents bought him forty years ago. Not quite grand, not quite modest. Just right. None of the furnishings or decoration had changed in all those years, except a new leather recliner in his study once a decade. At four hundred pounds he was not easy on the only item of furniture he used religiously every day.

Heller clicked off his vices in his mind. Food, drink, cigars, books, and work. Not bad, he thought. I have somehow avoided the two time-proven ways to pierce a man's fortress: women and money. He was not asexual or homosexual. Heller assumed he was heterosexual. But what he knew for certain was sex didn't have the same pull on him as it did for most men. In theory sex sounded wonderful. In his reality, it was rather uncomfortable and disconcerting. That's not something he shared publicly. People wouldn't understand. Thank God, his ex-wife was not the kind to air dirty laundry to the world.

Heller had reached out to Wannegrin almost nine months ago—long enough to have a baby—knowing the Jewish billionaire would help him even if it cost him a small fortune. Why was he so sure? Heller assumed that Wannegrin loathed Jonathan Alexander with every fiber of his being. Was it because Alexander was wealthier? That was conventional wisdom but Heller suspected it had to go deeper than that. Truly, it was not even guaranteed that Alexander was the wealthier of the two, no matter what the order *Forbes* listed them in. Both men had created a convoluted network of corporations to make it nearly impossible to discover just how much they were really worth.

Heller understood the value of keeping things unclear. His own role with the State Department was vague. He had reported to nine different men and women who held the title as Secretary of State. Not all were fans of his. One obvious reason was that as his legend grew, he sometimes reported directly to one of the six presidents he had served under. But none of the men or women he worked for ever dared raise a hand against him. It was known he was a genius. More importantly, it was known he was protected by his encyclopedic knowledge of the secrets of America's enemies—and friends.

No one knew if Heller was Democrat or Republican. Not even his parents ever knew how he voted. Heller was most comfortable being alone in the shadows and that's how he liked it and wanted to keep it. If the lights were turned on at his home, he intended to have a report or a book in hand to read, classical music playing in the background. Oh how the walls of his home had closed in on him during that awful year of marriage.

If your job was to be the official liaison between the various official security agencies of the United States Government—the FBI, the CIA, the NSA, the Defense Intelligence Agency, National Clandestine Service, the Office of Special Plans, and too many other three-letter offices and departments to count—it was much wiser to not advertise for the enemies of your nation that you might be the most important adversary they faced in the world. His administrative assistants—it took three to keep up with the outflow of his mind—and his other key underlings were instructed to gossip about his long three martini lunches—which wasn't always a lie—falling asleep in meetings—also not always a lie—his grumbling that no one knew what they were doing and never listened to him anyway, and his alarming memory lapses. Only the last rumor didn't have its roots in truth.

In the world of assessing threats and determining what agency or what person could best address it, he wanted the invisibility that accompanied being underestimated. If it was whispered in the halls of power that he was suffering from a combination of dementia, alcoholism, and failing kidneys, thus relegating him to the status of a has-been who didn't need to be monitored, so be it. The only time his reputation as an angry, forgetful sot had backfired on him was 9/11. The lesson he learned from that was that he had taken his cover so far that the one man who should have trusted and listened to him, ignored him. That would not show up in the history books.

From that moment on, he worked hard to make sure a few select levers of power inside and outside the government could be counted on to do his bidding, no questions asked. Wannegrin was one of those levers. He wasn't the only person Heller used when he wanted to make something happen that couldn't be attributed to the government, but Wannegrin was incredibly reliable.

Until now.

36

Sana'a, Yemen

THE IMAM WAS PLEASED. THE two minarets of the Great Mosque of Sana'a had sounded the call to worship and the faithful had thronged to stand and then bow shoulder to shoulder, united as brothers in worship and love of Allah. A few women worshiped in a curtained galley to prostrate themselves before Allah. That was acceptable, he thought, but most women, as was even more honorable and befitting, worshipped from home as the Prophet instructed.

The narrow streets of the Old City that fed into the plaza outside the Great Mosque were clogged with pedestrians to the point that it was nearly impossible to arrive in time for worship if one hadn't started early. Many men had to be turned away. They would be one part angry and one part sad. That was good. It showed the fervor of their devotion.

Let the casual and convenient Muslim—the kind that dishonored the Prophet and the devotion of true followers through lax morals and collaboration with the enemies of Allah—travel to the Saleh Mosque outside the city. The fact that it was named after a politician and not a great Imam descended from Mohammed; the fact that it allowed non Muslims inside not just as tourists but to observe worship; the fact that it was built as much for comfort and show as worship; that was all he needed to know about the state of spiritual affairs in Yemen. It was his job to remind men to live up to the meaning of the word Muslim: slave of God.

Those who have reinterpreted Muslim to mean a mere "follower" of Allah show, with their softening of the Prophet's words, their lack of commitment.

The Great Mosque was the first mosque built outside Mecca or Medina. Though some tried to explain otherwise, the Imam was convinced the Prophet of Allah ordained it. It housed the oldest extant copies of the Quran. Though not all agreed with him, he believed it was once a Byzantine cathedral, converted to the one true religion by Mohammed. That made the mosque even more beautiful in his eyes.

His sermon was short. Obey Allah. Flee corruption. Pursue holiness. Spread the beauty of Islam to the entire world by whatever means necessary. Whatever means. He preferred those means to be peaceful, but that was not always possible.

It was better to keep sermons short. That gave more time for the faithful to pray. That gave more time for the reading of the Quran.

As worship came to a close he smelled a trace of garlic in the air. Surely no one was cooking or had brought food inside the mosque. He would have to investigate and punish accordingly.

He watched with joy but a trace of concern as more than one thousand faithful took one last look toward the mihrab, the semicircular recess in the mosque that pointed to Qibla—the exact direction of Mecca.

Yes, I will investigate to see if anyone has defiled the mosque.

Anaheim, California

THE YOUNG BOY LET OUT a cry of wonder and amazement as purple, green, red, white, and other brightly colored streams and circles exploded over the Enchanted Castle at Wonder World. He was perched on his father's shoulders. He looked down as his mom comforted his little sister who was crying hysterically. The sound and lights scared her.

She is a big baby!

He looked back up and felt something much different. It was as if all the air had been sucked out of his lungs. A brilliant white light blinded him and sent stabbing arrows of excruciating pain into his mind. He felt his father begin to crumple beneath him. Sound came back as people all around him shrieked in horror.

He felt the first shards of metal rip into his body before there was nothing.

Bentonville, Arkansas

JUDY GARRISON WAS STRUGGLING TO fall asleep. She didn't like it when Dwight wasn't next to her. The love of her life. She kept hearing sounds as the little house creaked and groaned as wind and rain raged outside. She had gotten up once to get a glass of water and check all the locks on the doors. She got up a second time to check on the children. They were asleep but both four-year-old Dwight Jr. and seven-year-old Rebecca were tossing and turning. They must be feeling the same unease niggling at her.

What was going on with Dwight? He arranged for a guest preacher to take over the pulpit for at least the next two Sundays. He simply told her that she must trust him that there was something only he could do—but that he couldn't explain. But in Switzerland? He flew out of the Northwest Arkansas Regional Airport that morning for Atlanta. He would transfer to a Delta Boeing 777 flying to Zurich. He already had a train ticket from Zurich to Geneva. He had reservations at a modest hotel on the Bahnhofstrasse. He would call her to let her know he had arrived safe.

Dwight was the same as always, but in recent months had been secretive about some meetings he attended in Fayetteville. If she didn't trust him implicitly, she would have suspected he was having an affair. Not possible with her husband.

Judy turned over and suddenly sat up in bed. She smelled gas. She was sure everything was turned off in the kitchen.

As her feet hit the floor beside the queen size bed, she was tossed across the room as an explosion rocked the house. Her head broke a jagged hole in the drywall. Groggy, she scrabbled to her feet. She must save her children.

She stumbled to the door. Grasping the knob she felt the heat sear into the palm of her hand. She pulled it back with a piercing scream.

Then she was slammed back into the far wall of her room by a whoosh of ravenous flames.

As she felt her skin melting from her face, Judy thought first of the fires of Hell that had scared her so much as a child. Then her spirit embraced a divine light she knew must be heaven.

Various Cities, Europe

WITHIN THE SPACE OF AN hour, bombs ripped through nightclubs and discothèques in Berlin, Moscow, Turin, Milan, Paris, and London.

The carnage and death toll was devastating and the world was shocked as TV cameras projected young survivors huddled in blankets and rows of body bags lined on the streets of Europe's grand cities.

The tall man smiled as he watched coverage from a dingy flat in Milan, Italy. His apprentice was wrong. The world was paying attention. They had succeeded.

Donets'ka, Ukraine

THE FARMER LOOKED UP THROUGH the break of dawn to locate the sound of an airplane engine. A small cloud of orange dust trailed behind it, falling on his fields.

It was a chilly morning in Donets'ka.

Harvest was only a week away. What good could this magic fertilizer do in such a short time? The conditions of his crops didn't promise a great harvest, but he had seen worse. He was one of the few that balked at the offer of assistance from the International Farming Initiative. But how do you say no to the largesse offered by a department of the UN? That was what Vladimir Shavchuk, the man who had offered to buy his entire crop at a premium price had said. The farmer didn't like Shavchuk. He drove an expensive SUV and wore a fancy suit. It looked like he had his fingernails manicured at a salon. He had never tilled the earth. What would he know of the farming cycle? Fertilizer weeks before harvest?

The farmer didn't like the way the man smiled. He looked too confident and prosperous to work for the government, although most elected officials had a hand out for bribes.

The farmer doubted Shavchuk had ever set foot outside a big city, much less on a farm. He had tiptoed over broken stones and mud from his car to the front door, trying to keep his shiny leather shoes clean. He was pushy, even if his papers were in order, including a fancy document with a gold embossed FAO seal of the United Nations Food and Agriculture Organization.

But what could the farmer do? It was smarter to work with the FAO than demure; he might need their help in some future year if his fields failed to deliver a reasonable yield.

The farmer did what he knew he must do. He signed the papers and received a 10% deposit check. How did the man know how much the total yield would be for without first knowing his crop projections? He never even asked.

Shavchuk told the farmer to expect a crop duster in the next few weeks. That had been two weeks ago—and here it was, right on schedule. When was the government ever on schedule? This piqued his curiosity and suspicion even further.

The two men threw back shots of vodka and shook hands before Shavchuk left his house. The farmer watched him drive off. Afterward, the farmer called a few friends and acquaintances on farms in his region, all of who had received similar offers. What had the scientists come up with that was going to make them so much money they could throw *hryvnia* at them like it grew from trees? Maybe it will put us all out of business next year. How am I supposed to know these things?

His farm was relatively small. How big of checks had men like Nazarenko, Rudenko, and Vovk gotten? All had more than two thousand acre spreads.

Farming was all he knew. He didn't see how a newly discovered miracle fertilizer would increase his crop yield so close to harvest. But the premium being paid to test this dramatic new wonder product made resistance foolish and futile. He had already spent the deposit money on next year's seeds and a new engine for his decrepit combine. If his crop yield was greater than the Shavchuk's impromptu estimate, the man promised him a ten percent bonus on top of the premium.

Maybe his son could go to university in America and get out of this quagmire of political intrigue that the Russians—always the Russians—had created.

With rumors of more soldiers being deployed from Moscow, maybe it was time for the whole family to move to America. Years earlier, he had attended a trade show in Kremenchuk to look at impossibly expensive new farm equipment where he heard a professor of agriculture from the University of Nebraska speak through a translator.

What was the professor's name? He had repeatedly told his audience to just call him Bobby.

He liked him. He was real. Ever since that conference, he felt Nebraska would be a nice place to live. He watched the crop duster turn on its side as it circled back to lay another orangish cloud of its miracle load.

Just what did they think it could do this late in the harvest season?

37

Washington, D.C.

HELLER SAT IN HIS OFFICE. He and Marcum returned to D.C. on a military chopper after his dinner with Walter Wannegrin. He rarely slept more than four hours a night. Tonight he would not sleep at all. Reports kept arriving on the secure line. What was going on? This was orchestrated chaos.

Al Qaeda? ISIS? Of course. But in the pit of his enormous gut, he somehow sensed that the series of macabre events went deeper.

He picked up the phone and made a quick call, giving a terse command: "Move on the son."

"We don't know if the kid is right for the job."

"Doesn't matter," Heller said. "He's all we got."

"You gave us a week to get to know him."

"We don't have a week," Heller said. "Get him reconnected with Anderson, now," he ordered before cutting the line.

Heller sighed. So much to do, so little time. He considered the levers available to him. Until he did further research, Wally would be put on the bench. But if he couldn't trust his longest friend in the world, Walter Wannegrin, who could he trust?

New York City

"SO YOU DIDN'T KNOW YOUR classmate at NYU, Jason Anderson, was Jonathan Alexander's son?" Greene asked.

"Of course not," Patrick Wheeler answered. "I thought Alexander's son was killed in a car crash. Is this some sort of a game?"

"Do we look like we play games?" Green asked. "Tell us again how well you know Anderson."

"Like I said, we had a couple classes and a couple drinks together. He wasn't very outgoing—not sure how many friends he had—but he seemed like a regular guy. I knew he wasn't hurting for cash, but he sure didn't act like he was the son of one of the richest men in the world."

"How good of friends were you?"

"Jason and me? I don't know. When you are grinding through grad school, you sort of get close to people. You form a bond. But I haven't talked to him in a year. Not since graduation. So it's probably safer to say we weren't BFFs."

"What is a BFF?" Agent Greene asked suspiciously.

Really? There's someone that doesn't know what a BFF is?

Before he could enlighten Greene, Rasmussen interjected, "Best friends forever."

Wheeler looked in surprise at the man that he had named "the Sphinx" in his mind. So he can speak. I do wonder if these guys have first names. Or maybe the FBI only hires guys who are named Agent. Will I have to legally change my name if this conversation is going where I think it is?

"But you have his cell and email in your phone?"

"Yes. Yes. I've told you that a bunch of times."

"Just wanted to make sure I am getting things right," Greene answered.

"Did you put other classmates in your contact list?" Rasmussen asked. "Or just BFFs?"

"Some. Sure. Not everyone."

What was this? BFF? That sounds creepy coming from Agent Rasmussen.

"And he never reached out to you since graduation?" Greene asked in a slightly different form for the fifth or sixth time.

"If he did, I missed the call."

"Never?"

"No!"

A little more than a day after entering his apartment to discover two FBI agents sitting in the tiny living room of his apartment, he still hadn't returned to work or been in contact with KPMG.

This better be legitimate or I'm officially unemployed.

Wheeler wondered for the hundredth time if this really was a job interview. He kept a steady banter of protest going, reminding the agents he had a great job and was up for a promotion, but truth was, he was intrigued. He was going nowhere fast with KPMG so a change was welcome. Becoming an FBI agent? That held an incredible, almost irresistible, allure to it. But being grilled around the clock felt all wrong. So he kept fighting his two interrogators, who more and more felt like captors.

Why do I feel like I'm being looked at as a suspect in a crime?

He had spent almost twenty-four hours in a nice but nondescript conference room in the Financial District. It looked like you would expect an FBI conference room to look. The wood grained laminate table, like everything else, looked good but not too good. Leather or more likely some synthetic leather chairs were comfortable and practical. The only breaks they gave him were to eat sub sandwiches and heed the call of nature. Wheeler felt sweaty and dirty. He longed for a shower and change of clothes. His pants felt glued to his skin. He was exhausted—Agents Greene and Rasmussen looked like they were just getting started.

Is this a test?

Wheeler decided that no matter how alluring a job with the FBI might seem, he was done spilling his guts to these guys. He let the silence extend. Were they waiting for him to say something else? Was there something he was supposed to add? Had he said something wrong?

He opened his mouth to say more, but told himself, just shut up and wait. Then he felt a flicker and remembered something. He had seen Jason.

"I did see Jason once this past summer."

The two agents looked at him impassively. Did they already know that?

"I forgot because it was only in passing and we didn't get a chance to talk."

"Go on."

"He was leaving a bar while I was going in."

"And?"

"Simple as that. He was with a group of friends. I had worked late—and drank a little too much that night. That's why I forgot."

"Remembering anything else Patrick?" asked Greene, the man who had conducted most of the interview the entire time.

"No. That's it. All we did was nod at each other."

"Name of the bar?"

"The Cutting Room. It's on 26th."

Wheeler braced himself for an hour of grueling, grinding questions to elucidate this chance encounter with a former classmate who looked like anything but the son of a multi, multi billionaire. But no one said anything for a moment. Then a door opened. A man entered and placed a briefcase on the middle of the table. He unsnapped two side fasteners and opened the lid of the hard-shelled thin, classic case that you only saw in movies from the 60s and second hand stores. Maybe I have entered the Twilight Zone, Patrick thought.

The new man pulled out a document that was at least fifteen pages long and slid it across the table to Wheeler.

"Read it, please," was all he said.

"Is this a job offer?"

"Read it."

Greene and Rasmussen watched him expressionlessly.

Patrick looked at the stoic agents. He would find no clues to what was on the paper from these two.

What a strange turn of events. Who would have ever guessed that Jason Anderson was the son of a billionaire?

He started reading. If the document in front of him could be believed, he was going to be paid a lot of money as an independent contractor to attempt to reconnect with him—and spy on the son of one of the richest men in the world.

Could that be true?

He started over at the first page and read every word carefully a second time.

Washington, D.C.

Gwen Hampton twirled a strand of hair with her forefinger. She pulled the tress into a straight line and examined the black and white streaks. To color or not to color? Once you started down that road, it was a commitment to one more task on the to-do list.

She was disappointed in Markham's report. If she was to go to the president to let him know that Jonathan Alexander was a threat to national and global security, she needed more than the the bits and pieces Markham overheard and brought to her.

She knew she shouldn't, but after watching five TV monitors with alarming events for the past few hours, she couldn't resist. She pulled the emergency pack of Kools from her bottom left desk drawer. She popped a cigarette from the pack, lit it with a cheap Bic lighter with Betty Boop on it, and inhaled deeply. How far behind was the vodka she kept hidden behind the ice cube trays in the kitchenette of her office suite?

Los Angeles. Turin. London. Moscow. Berlin. Paris.

Why did she suspect that these were just preliminaries and the real carnage was to follow?

Then there was the question of Emanuel Heller. He was on to something and up to something. He was involved with Jonathan Alexander in some way. Hopefully on the side of the angels, she thought.

Markham confirmed as much, but added no details or insights.

Hampton had near-unfettered access to the president, but it wouldn't stay that way if she bugged him with rumors that may lead to nothing more than rabbit trails. He was a hunter and had made it clear, he didn't want to shoot rabbits; he was only interested in the big game.

Bring her suspicions on Alexander organizing mass chaos or sit and listen while others speculated?

Time to go home. She might not get any sleep, but at least she could catch a shower.

Thirty minutes later Gwen Hampton's neighborhood was rocked when four pounds of c4 exploded as she opened her back entry door.

Her husband was on business in Kansas City. He was rushed to the Richards-Gebaur Air Reserve Station and flown to D.C. in the co-pilot's seat of a Convair F-106 at a speed of more than 1,500 miles-per-hour.

He was not brought to the morgue to identify his wife's body. There was nothing left of her to identify.

38

The Isle of Patmos

CLAIRE STEVENS SAT ON THE balcony of her apartment overlooking the Aegean Sea. She nibbled from a small plate of fruit and cheese. She took another sip of Chardonnay. She had expected to be with Nicky. He sent her a cryptic message that he was treading water and it would be awhile before he saw her again. Nothing else. No "I miss you" or explanation.

She didn't know if that made her angry or hurt her feelings. Cynically, it just confirmed that men were often inconsiderate brutes. Except her father. He was definitely the exception. The problem was she didn't think she could be attracted to a man like her father. It was men like Nicky that stirred her passions.

Or could it be that it was Nicky, the crown prince and heir of Patmos, who singularly awakened desire in her?

All she could do now was wait for the Sana'a results. When she told the scientific team the name she had given to the Chimera, they were curious as to the meaning behind Mariama. Patton and Dolzhikov laughed at her sentimentality. Starnes started to make a joke out of it, saw her expression, and said in his folksy Middle America vernacular: "Hot damn, Dr. Claire, I think you picked a winner. Mariama has a sweet ring to my ears."

That was it. Mariama it was. That pleased her, but she couldn't show it. One thing Claire could not stand was not being taken seriously in the first place.

Claire felt restless. She stood up and leaned over the rail. Had she done the right thing? What would her parents think if she explained why she had done it? Would they even let her explain?

She looked at the distant waters. Patmos was the ark. Soon the waters that teemed with death would rise and begin to flood the earth. Not all of it. Just the parts that needed to be cleansed. According to Nicky, speaking with too much wine in him, Asia, Africa, and the Middle East were targeted for the brunt of the mass executions. Asia because of its uncontrollable population growth; Africa because of its brutality and to give unfettered access to its abundant resources; the Middle East because of its religiously motivated designs on world domination—a rigid world where progress and enlightenment went to die.

Central and South America would be hit more strategically. Drug fields and centers of drug traffic would be eviscerated—the everyday people would stand up and call what they did to these predators blessed. Massive slums from Mexico City to Buenos Aires would be decimated by bombs, disease, and famine. Borders to the West would be barred shut with walls and armies. Progressive countries of culture would be preserved as much as possible.

What of Israel? Could it be quarantined from the holocaust around it?

"My uncle has made a deal," Nicky had told her. "If terms of the deal are maintained, the country will be protected. If not; all bets are off."

"I thought Israel was where the Battle of Armageddon was to take place in End Times prophecy," she pointed out to Nicky. "If your uncle is to be the Beast, doesn't that mean Israel becomes a battlefield."

"He doesn't believe in all that stuff literally," Nicky responded. "He just likes the the poetry of the concept. He does intend to build heaven on earth. The plans he has to move resources to the survivors are genius."

"So why all the attacks in Europe and the United States?"

"He knows he must show the West in small measure what would be done to them if the barbarians had the means to do so. He is assuaging their collective conscience on the part they must play to facilitate the removal of those who bring nothing but misery to the world—and getting their own homes in order."

Claire slid the balcony door back and walked to the small bathroom. She opened the cabinet behind the mirror and selected the unmarked brown bottle that contained 90 Pristiq pills she had not used since joining The Aristotle Research Company, the shell that provided cover for Patmos.

Nicky's terse note had worked itself inside the whorls and valleys of her brain. Did she need one now? She hesitated. Taking 50mg of the square brown Pristiq tablet would undoubtedly take the edge off the angry rumbling that was welling inside her, but even if Pfizer promised otherwise, it also took the edge off her best thinking. Her choice since grad school at University of Chicago, at least in her mind, had always come down a simple question: Do you want to be brilliant or happy?

She put the bottle back on the shelf. Patmos was the most effective drug she had ever taken and she wanted to keep it that way. Brilliance was what mattered in the grand scheme of saving the planet.

The first phase had begun. The rise of the Beast. This was a moment to savor fully.

She stepped back outside. Somewhere in the darkness Claire sensed a presence. Her mind went back to Mariama and all the other prepubescent girls she wanted to avenge. She was doing it for their future—even if many would not be alive to experience it personally. Like Mariama they would be dead, but no longer victims of paternalistic societies that brutalized the weak—especially the female weak.

When Claire called a colleague to find out how Mariama, the girl, not the Chimera, was doing she was given the news that her father had killed her shortly after the family visited the GlobalHope mobile clinic.

Only a few short weeks before hearing the news, Claire's heart would be broken. She would cry herself to sleep at night for months. But that wasn't the case with Mariama's death. There would be no grieving. Claire had no time for tears. Her heart was already set on the direction her life must go. She would make sure that Mariama never truly died.

Are you watching me now, Mariama? Do you know I am doing this for you?

Claire felt a little better. As she watched distant wave caps, some of the melancholy she was feeling lifted. She was doing the right thing. She was sure. It was for a little girl in a remote village of Guinea, Africa, who was floating in and out of the lungs of worshipers in Sana'a, and who would soon be introduced to others through the sharing of human fluids and other contact—and applications to population centers that were more than a whisper.

How many? How far would Mariama travel? Would she cling to life as she took it?

Stay alive, Mariama, Claire murmured. Do your work. Help me create a new world.

39

New York City

BURKE FORCED HIS EYES FROM the gruesome death of Henri on the small screen of his iPad and brought his mind back to the present.

"Why are we exiting here?" Burke asked his cabby.

Middle Easterner? Hispanic? Russian? The man hadn't said a word during the drive so it was hard to tell.

"Dispatch said bad traffic on the Van Wyck closer to airport. I know a back way to get you there early with no trouble."

Traffic didn't look bad as they exited a couple miles before JFK. But road conditions changed fast in a metropolitan with twenty million residents and another three million visitors.

The driver had been relatively cautious on the highway, but now that he was on Jamaica Avenue, he started accelerating, weaving through light evening traffic, and braking hard at traffic signals like you would expect an old school New York City taxi driver to do.

What the heck? Burke wondered, his antennae suddenly up and alert to danger.

As they approached the intersection of Jamaica and Merrick, the driver powered around the corner, throwing Burke to the side. He raced past two side streets and suddenly slammed on the brakes. Burke's head hit the Plexiglas divider between front and back seats.

The left and right doors were thrown open before the car came to a complete stop and two crew cut men were on top of him by the time he was leaning back in his seat and reaching to feel if his forehead was bleeding.

Lightly dazed, Burke still had his fighter's wits and threw an elbow at the windpipe of the man on his left while he cranked a head butt at the man to his right. Both blows landed but the quarters were so tight the blows lacked incapacitating effect.

Both men were methodically trying to control Burke's hands—a good sign or a bad sign flashed through Burke's mind, realizing that if they had come to kill him he would already be dead—as he fought frantically to keep his hands free. He heard a sliding sound. Risking a glance forward, he saw the cab driver leaning through the window with a hypodermic needle. They didn't come to kill him. They came to do to him what was done to Henri. Last chance he thought.

He seemed to relax as the needle was brought toward his shoulder. Then Burked exploded forward catching the driver on the bridge of his nose with the crown of his head in a nasty head snap. He wrenched left on top of one of his assailants, with the man on his right still gripping his wrist and being yanked along with the move. The driver tried one last stab with the needle, but Burke's maneuver made him miss, and the cabbie stuck the point in the middle of the man on his right's back. The attacker immediately slumped forward, almost instantly becoming dead weight on Burke's back. One down, two to go.

The man beneath him had Burke's wrist in a death grip and was twisting. The driver was not a trained fighter and his attempts to punch Burke were either absorbed by the man slumped on his back or were too weak to matter.

Burke sank his teeth into the left cheek of the man beneath him, his immediate threat, opening and closing his mouth to get closer to the eye orbit. He didn't like the rusty taste of human blood any more than the average man on the street, but he was willing to do anything to survive—and avenge Pauline and Henri. The man broke off his viselike grip on Burke's wrist to defend his face. That gave Burke the break he needed to arch back and using a combination of weight and power plant his right palm into the man's solar plexus, driving the air from his lungs. Both of Burke's hands shot up to the outside of the man's neck where he expertly found the pressure points for the carotid artery and clamped onto a sleeper hold as hard as he dared. He didn't want to kill the man by crushing his larynx, just get him to fall asleep so he could take him somewhere to interview him. The man's face was a mess, blood flowing into his mouth and down his neck as his eyes bulged from lack of oxygen to the brain.

Where was the cab driver? He might have another needle.

Burke let go of the man, bucked the man behind him off his back, opened the left door, and stumbled out of the cab to find the driver and assess his next move.

The barrel of a silencer mounted on a Sig Sauer was pointed at his forehead.

Two familiar intense dark blue eyes stared at him, giving a simple command without a word spoken: Don't move or you're dead.

Behind those eyes was the man who had changed the course of Burke's life. Colonel Arnold—just call me Arnie—Grayson.

Burke remembered words his grandma had spoken to him on many occasions: "No matter how far away from God you've run … you're never too far away to pray."

Grayson was joined by three more armed men. Nope. Grayson wasn't there to kill him. At least not immediately. That was bad news. Burke's pain tolerance was off the charts. But Grayson already knew that. That was even worse news.

I am indeed far away from God, Burke thought. But I think it's time to pray.

40

Alexandria, Virginia

THE ORDERS WERE CLEAR. No more live meetings until Alexander declared otherwise.

But could Alexander be trusted? Was he capable of command? Perhaps it was time for new leadership.

Walter Wannegrin hesitated another moment, staring blankly at the flashing cursor on the black screen.

Yes, change was needed.

He typed three sentences giving the place and time for the next gathering of the chosen few. He paused again. Would they rally to him? If not, his life was finished. What of his dreams for his country? At the end of the day that was the only reason he had thrown in his lot with Alexander.

He sighed and hit send

I'm sorry Emanuel. You would never understand what I am doing. But the world has changed. All we've worked for to bring peace and prosperity is on the brink of collapse. New measures are needed. Even if Alexander is wrong on many things, he is right on a few things that must happen if civilization is to survive.

41

New York City

BURKE WOKE WITH A PAINFUL start. He couldn't move. He took quick inventory. His arms and legs were strapped to a forged iron chair. He rocked his body weight back and forth and tried to move it. It was bolted to the floor. He was naked and cold. He was sitting in absolute darkness. His eyelids were taped wide open.

He rotated his neck left and right. He clinched his hands into fists and felt a mixture of pain and tingling as blood tried to find its way back into areas that were nearly numb from lack of circulation. He tested his restraints. No movement. There was little wiggle room, literally or metaphorically.

Suddenly he was blinded by a floodlight shown directly on his face. Tears flooded from the corners of his eyes as he futilely tried to clench them shut against the blinding pain.

He heard footsteps approach him.

"I hope you slept well," Colonel Grayson said quietly. "It may be awhile before you sleep again."

"I should have killed you," Burke spat out.

"But you didn't so here we are. Together again."

"What do you want with me?"

"You know what I want from you and you know what I'm willing to do to you to help you speak. But why bore you with details, most of which you can guess, based on your position. I'll just offer you one preview of coming attractions. I need to know where the upload you were supposed to send only me is, and how many total hosts there are."

"I should have known you were involved. This operation stunk from day one."

"But, again, you didn't know and so here we are together to have an intimate little chat."

"I'll talk if you talk."

"No doubt, you'll talk. Maybe I'll talk. But that depends on my mood, not your threats. Really Burke. When did you become so melodramatic? This seems beneath one of the finest natural born killers I ever commanded."

"You apparently didn't train me well enough."

"That's obvious. Or I would be dead. I would ask why you didn't do the smart thing and off me, but we're short on time."

"So what did you do with the girl?"

"By girl, do you mean Pauline? Or perhaps you are remembering Breshna."

Burke let out a guttural snarl and struggled against his restraints with every ounce of strength he possessed. He pitched his weight forward and backward, and side to side, but the chair was anchored securely and he was merely wasting precious energy. He suddenly felt a jolt of electricity course through his body. His muscles cramped painfully against the restraints.

Grayson laughed.

"That's only 50 thousand volts, Burke. Same as what the police use with a Taser. If you want to be petulant and churlish over things that are in the distant past, keep going. There's plenty more volts where that came from."

Burke glared at him defiantly, but in his heart and mind, he knew Grayson would eventually break him. No one could withstand unrestrained torture. Sooner or later, he—or whatever was left of him—would tell Grayson everything he wanted to know.

"You always did have a soft spot in your heart for stray cats Lieutenant Burke. Perhaps Breshna was truly as sweet as she seemed and worthy of your chivalry. You should have known better. You don't get romantically involved with an Iraqi girl when you are fighting the Iraqis. I understand your sudden disappearance hurt her deeply. I would know. I did most of the hurting. It was quite unpleasant. I hate to be the one to break something else to you, Lieutenant. Your meeting with Pauline at the Hotel Hassler in Rome was not by chance. You just aren't very lucky at love, are you soldier? Before we get down to the real business at hand, I wanted you to know that."

Burke slowed his breathing down to calm himself. He sighed and resigned himself to what awaited him his last few hours of his failed life.

If there really is a heaven and hell is it too late to pray?

The Story Continues

Coming August 2016

The Voice of the Dragon
The Patmos Conspiracy Book 2

Then I saw another beast come up out of the earth. He had two horns like those of a lamb, but he spoke with the voice of a dragon.
Revelation 13:11, NLT

About the Author

MARK "M.K." GILROY is author of the #1 bestselling Kristen Conner Mystery Series. He is a veteran publishing executive who has acquired, developed, authored, and ghostwritten numerous books that have sold millions of copies and landed on various bestseller lists.

Rise of the Beast is the first of five books in the Patmos Conspiracy Series.

He and his wife Amy recently became empty nesters with the youngest of six off to college. They reside in Brentwood, Tennessee.

www.markgilroy.com
www.facebook.com/MKGilroy.Author

CPSIA information can be obtained
at www.ICGtesting.com
Printed in the USA
LVOW04s2108171116
513437LV00012B/554/P